HIDDEN MATE

THE WOLF BORN TRILOGY

JEN L. GREY

CHAPTER ONE

"This is everything," Brock said as he set my pink luggage on the ground. He focused his silver eyes on me and ran a hand through his messy chestnut-brown hair. In the right light, hints of auburn were visible, but not in the dim dorm room. He pulled his navy button-down shirt over his gray slacks.

He'd be attractive if I didn't find him downright repulsive. He was the typical elitist jerk who came with the territory of alpha heirs. He wasn't part of my pack but rather part of the second strongest pack that happened to have the most money. He played the part of a snob very well.

"Hey, I still have a few bags downstairs." Roxy threw her long red hair over her shoulder and pouted. "Can you get those?" She batted her hazel eyes at him like that would change his answer.

I used the pack bond to link to my best friend. *Don't encourage him. It's bad enough that Dad said I could only come to Kortright University with him.* In fact, it was odd. If he thought there was any chance of me and Brock getting together, he would be disappointed. I couldn't mate with someone who thought they were better than everyone else. I refused to.

"It sucked carrying up Sadie's, so get yours yourself." He pointed at the plywood door. "I need to get settled into my own room, anyway."

"Don't you have someone taking care of that for you?" Roxy pointed at her white, flowy top and black miniskirt and then lifted her right foot in the air, emphasizing her black strappy heels. "I could really use your help. I'm wearing a dress and heels."

"Change, then," he said hatefully and turned his attention back to me. "I still don't understand why you hang out with someone like her." He scowled at her.

"And I don't see why you agreed to come here ..." She paused and held up a finger. "Oh, wait, I do. You wanna get in her pants."

Oh, my God. Kill me now.

"Like I said, you're a really classy girl to be friends with." Brock stepped toward her and snarled. "Why don't you take your pathetic ass back home?"

Her breathing became ragged, and her eyes glowed faintly. "What did you just call me?"

"You two, stop it." They'd argued the entire way here. He and his driver picked us up in his expensive Navigator while someone who worked for his family had come here to set up his dorm room for him. "It'll be a long year otherwise."

"Well, if she respected—" he started, and my wolf surged forward.

My skin tingled, alerting me that my fur was about to sprout. "She's my best friend—end of story." I hated that alphas tried to tell you what to do in every aspect of your life. My dad bullied me almost every day, and this was why

I'd wanted to go away to college so damn badly. It was a chance to find myself.

"We'll see how long that lasts," he murmured and then straightened, focusing on me. "I'll be by here in a couple of hours to grab you for dinner."

I wanted to tell him to fuck off, but that wouldn't go over well. For whatever reason, Brock was the cost of my college experience and freedom. I had no clue why, but I couldn't push too hard too soon or it could all be ripped away from me. "Okay."

I turned my back on him and scanned the room. It wasn't huge like my room back home, but it was big enough. Twin beds sat across from each other against the light gray walls with an end table on both sides. A small window was right in the center of the beds and overlooked the tall brick building that housed the school library.

At the end of each bed sat a small metal desk. I unzipped one of my bags, pulled out the down mattress topper, and tucked it into the corners. It wasn't much, but I'd sleep more peacefully here than I ever had back home. Here, I wouldn't be under Dad's constant scowl or watchful eyes.

Well ... that was a stretch. Brock would be doing just that, but at least, I didn't have to deal with my father's constant nagging over why I couldn't be a better shifter or complaining that I wasn't born male. He wanted an alpha heir, and with me being a woman, I was disqualified even though people pretended otherwise. So, my responsibility was to mate with an alpha heir that could rule over both his pack and mine when the time came.

The door shut, and Brock's overly musky smell thinned. All shifters had a hint of musk to their scent, but he wore musky cologne on top of it to make his scent even stronger. Like that would prove he was more powerful or something.

"He really is an asshole." Roxy frowned and sat on the bed to remove her heels. "I mean, he carried all of your bags up here and then talked to me like that."

She shouldn't have been surprised. She was from my pack and had to deal with the same dictator. However, her dad wasn't like that with her family, which was a shocker. Granted, he was low on the totem pole, so that might have explained it. However, those low-hanging fruits, or anyone who talked ill of my dad, sometimes conveniently disappeared.

"Look, I'll come and help you." I picked up some clothes I had on hangers and walked over to the small closet in front of the bed. When I opened the door, I found a full-length mirror attached to the back of it. I hung up the clothes and looked at myself in the mirror.

My rose-gold hair caught my attention immediately. Most people thought it was dyed, but it wasn't. The soft pink color was natural and highlighted my light ocean-blue eyes. Standing at five foot eight, I wasn't tall by shifter stan-dards but taller than most human girls.

"You'd think he'd try to take care of your best friend too," she whined. "It's like he already thinks he owns you."

I agreed, and that was a huge problem. "We both know he doesn't give a shit about me. He only wants to earn points with my father."

"Your dad is the wolf king." Roxy wrinkled her nose as she put on socks. "I mean ... even some of the other super-naturals cower in fear. Hell, if I didn't know he was such a dick to you, I'd be trying to get in his good graces as well."

"You should still try." I always worried that something bad

would happen to her because of me. He hated weak supernaturals and wanted me to only associate with the cream of the crop. The fact that my best friend was below our status pissed him off. I had a feeling he would use her against me one day, so sucking up to him would be a good thing for her and her family.

Even though my father might not like me, I was the closest thing he had to an heir. I was his first born, which was my only saving grace. He'd gone through so many women, trying to birth a son, but they'd all come out as girls. It was poetic justice. Not that it mattered because he'd always cast them out of the pack like garbage. He said having one bitch was enough. The worst part was that both the mother and daughter would die shortly after in some sort of freak accident. Anyone he found worthless tended to disappear or die. "You never know when you might need his favor."

"Nope, anyone who makes my girl feel like a piece of shit is not cool with me." She slipped on her black tennis shoes and closed her eyes. "I can't believe Brock's making me do this."

"Don't be so dramatic." I tried to hold back my laughter. "Wearing tennis shoes isn't nearly as bad as you're making it out to be." I gestured to my own feet.

"You can pull off the cute, girl-next-door vibe." She stood and pointed at her outfit. "This is the sexy vixen look, and anything but strappy heels really takes away from the ensemble."

"Stop complaining." I wore a black shirt and jean shorts just for the purpose of moving in. "That outfit won't work for getting things in order anyway."

"It will too." She walked to the door and opened it. "I'm wearing this to the Student Center tonight. There will be hot guys there, and I need to make sure I get my pick of the litter."

Now that the door was open, we had to be careful about what we said. Humans weren't allowed to know about our kind. *You do realize you can't have relations with a human.* Dad made it clear that choosing a human as a mate equaled a death sentence. They were the worst of the worst, the weakest of the weak. *That would be a problem.*

That's having a relationship with one, and I wasn't really talking about a human, anyway. She shut the door behind us and waggled her brows. *I want one I can be rough with and not get tied down to. Maybe a vampire or something that isn't a shifter. When we get home, we'll have to either find our fated mates or search for a chosen one. I just want to have fun while we're here.*

We passed through the hallway, dodging shrieking girls. Most of them were sophomores who were obviously excited to see each other after a long summer break. Their squeals hurt my sensitive ears, but I forced myself not to react.

We rode the elevator down to the bottom floor, and my eyes went straight to the outdoors. The school was located in Hidden Ridge, Tennessee, about two hours away from Nashville where my dad resided. "Why don't we walk around the campus while Brock is preoccupied?"

She stomped her feet a few times and blew out a breath. "I'm not appropriately—"

"Please." I pouted. My wolf wanted to get outside. "This may be my only chance ..."

Her body sagged as if it hurt her to agree. "Fine, but only because I don't like him."

"Good enough for me." It had been a fifty-fifty shot with her, so this made me very happy. "Let's go." I took her hand and dragged her into the main lobby.

The university was a small, private school that catered to the rich, but also offered limited scholarships to under-privileged families. This was the school Dad had graduated from, and he wanted me to follow in his footsteps. I'd have loved to go to the University of Knoxville or something, but it wasn't an option. So, I'd taken what I could get.

As we stepped into the lobby, the modernity of it all still surprised me. Lights hung down from the ceiling every few feet, and the walls were painted a medium gray. A cluster of leather couches sat in the center, creating a huge square in primary colors to offset the walls. Groups of girls sat around on all of the couches, catching up.

At least, they weren't shrieking.

Roxy looked at a girl with a clipboard and gestured to her standard black luggage. "I still have those two suitcases. Is it okay if I leave them here while I grab a snack at the Student Center?"

"Sure." The girl waved her hand at all of the boxes scattered across the room. "It'll be fine just as long as everything is up by six."

"It will be." I smiled and pulled Roxy after me.

"You must know how much I love you for doing this." She looped her arm through mine, and we walked outside. The girls' dorm was located between the large brick Student Center and the huge building that contained both the library and gym.

The campus sat on over a hundred acres of land with woods surrounding it. That was one benefit of going here: there was room to run when our wolves got too restless.

It was around four, and the sun was still high in the sky. The southern heat was brutal, but the nature around here couldn't be beat.

We walked along the white concrete sidewalk between

the two buildings. Several groups hung out at the benches, and three huge oak trees shaded the entire area.

As we got closer, a sweet scent hung in the air. That only meant one thing. *A vampire is nearby.*

Roxy sniffed the air. *More than one.*

I wanted to kill her. *Could you be any more obvious?*

Oh, stop being dramatic. She rolled her eyes. *No one is paying attention to us.*

Two girls turned toward us and away from the two people they'd been talking to. The scent grew stronger, and I knew exactly who the vampires were.

The taller girl, with her black hair cut in a bob like mine, examined us. It almost felt like she was plotting her next meal. She had the gothic look down pat, and the thick eyeliner brought out her dark brown eyes. There was a faint hint of red in her irises, but nothing a human would notice.

A smirk spread across the other girl's face, and her inky, brown eyes practically glowed. Her long chocolate hair fell over her shoulders. She was shorter than her friend by at least two inches, but she bore a more natural look.

They're the vampires. Even though supernatural races mixed, we tended to keep to our own kind. At least, in my father's pack, we did.

Let's get out of here. Roxy's discomfort radiated through our pack link. *The less we're around them, the better.*

Wait. I had to give her hell as I allowed her to lead us toward the edge of the benches where two men sat across the walkway at a table. *What happened to having some sexy time with vampires?*

Shut it. She glanced back over her shoulder at them. *First off, they're girls, and I don't swing that way; and secondly, I've never been around them before. Consider my previous statement retracted. Maybe I can find a sexy shifter here.*

That was for the best. We didn't need her inviting trouble into our lives more than we already had. Vampires could be sneaky and tempting. We slid onto the bench away from the others, and I felt a cold chill run down my spine. Those vamps were still watching us.

Holy shit. Roxy gasped. *Look at the two dudes right next to us.*

I tried to be subtle and pretended to gaze around the campus. One of the guys ran his hand across his buzzed hair and smiled. He was attractive, but my attention flicked to his friend.

Navy blue eyes met mine, making me uncomfortable. I wanted to run my hands through his shaggy jet-black hair. He nibbled on his bottom lip. A tribal tattoo peeked out from under his shirt sleeve, and I had to fight the urge to walk over and trace it with my finger.

I took a deep breath, and the solid truth hit me hard in my chest. He smelled of summer rain, which smelled even better than normal humans. There wasn't a strong musky animal smell to him. Dammit, I needed to rein in my attraction to him.

"Sadie." Brock's nasally, entitled voice broke whatever spell that was holding me.

When I didn't respond, he grabbed my arm painfully and growled, "What are you doing out here?"

CHAPTER TWO

B rock's face turned red. "I told you I'd be by to get you for dinner in a few hours." He motioned back to the girls' dorm. "That meant you weren't supposed to leave."

I hated being manhandled. "Stop it." If I didn't stand up for myself now, it would only get worse.

His silver eyes took on a slight glow. "You disobeyed me."

"Dude, you're not her ..." Roxy trailed off, conscious of the humans around. "... boyfriend."

His grip tightened. "Is that what it'll take for her to listen to me?"

"No, it won't." I pulled my arm from his grasp and lifted my chin. "You need to calm down. I don't answer to you."

"Hey," a stern female voice called from behind him, and a sweet scent hit my nose harder.

Brock spun around to face the two vampires heading our way. "Can I help you?"

"Yeah, you can." The gothic one nodded toward the humans. "You need to chill. You're making a scene."

His eyes narrowed as he sucked in a deep breath. "I think you need to mind your own business."

"We only came out here to relax and get some air." Maybe I could reason with him. A few humans were already glancing our way. "School starts tomorrow, so we wanted to get the lay of the land."

"Besides, aren't you supposed to get working in your room?" Roxy lifted an eyebrow and crossed her arms. "Why are you even outside?"

"I was getting a few things from the car and noticed you two weren't in your dorm room where you were supposed to be." His jaw clenched.

"Nope, we decided to go outside to enjoy the sunshine." I couldn't help but glance back at the two guys across the way.

I shouldn't have. Dreamy looked at me with such disgust.

I couldn't blame him, though. The fact that Brock manhandled me like I was a piece of property and I kind of let him spoke volumes. I needed to figure a way out of whatever arrangement we had going on here.

"Fine," he conceded. "Stay away from everyone else."

We all knew what he meant by that—humans. *Slick* wasn't his middle name. "Got it."

He glanced at the two vampires still standing close to us before walking away. "See you in a few hours."

"Well, isn't he just pleasant?" The more natural vamp sat beside me and straightened out her white, flowery dress. "Is he your boyfriend?"

"God, no," I said a little too loudly. "Don't even try to curse me with that."

"Maybe you aren't as much of a pushover as I thought."

The one dressed all in black sat next to Roxy. "Dude, you're wearing tennis shoes with that outfit?"

"Don't get me started." Roxy rubbed between her eyes with her pointer finger. "I had on sexy, black, strappy heels, but someone convinced me to put on tennis shoes to carry up luggage. Next thing I know, I'm out here." *You don't think they'll bite us, right?*

I bit my bottom lip, trying not to laugh. *I'd say no since humans are present. They did just get on Brock for making a scene.* Sometimes, Roxy was a tad paranoid.

True. She glanced at the vamp's black skirt, which was similar to hers. "You have good taste."

The main difference between the two outfits was the vamp's dressy, black tank top.

"My name's Lillith," the gothic vampire said, and then she pointed at her friend. "And that is Katherine."

They were being nice, which caught me off guard. My dad painted them as cold-hearted villains. "Uh ... I'm Sadie." My voice went up at the end.

A predatory smile crossed Lillith's face. "Is that your name, or are you asking us?"

"It's her name." Roxy snorted. "And I'm Roxy."

"Are you both from ..." Katherine paused. "The same area?"

Being around humans could be problematic. "Yeah, we are. Our parents live in the same neighborhood." It was common knowledge that packs moved into neighborhoods and lived side by side. Most supernaturals bought whole plots of land and hired contractors to build the homes. In our case, my great grandfather had been an architect and builder for hundreds of supernatural families. It was easier to work with our own kind. It's one reason my family became the most influential pack in America. It also helped that they had a blueprint for every supernatural house or business in America.

"And I'm assuming Dumbass is too." Lillith waved her hand toward the still retreating Brock.

"Nope, actually, he's not." My body sagged before I could stop it. "He's a family friend." I guessed that was the best way to put it. Brock's dad was rubbing elbows with my dad, hoping to team up with him.

Tall, dark, and sexy keeps glancing over at you. Roxy linked with me, amusement on her face. *Too bad he and his friend are human.*

Tell me about it. This was the most interested I'd ever been in someone, and I hadn't even gotten within five feet of him. *They're human, and we'd better keep our distance. The last thing we need is Brock causing problems.*

And he would in a heartbeat, Roxy agreed and focused back on the vampires. "Aren't you two night owls or something?"

"Eh, we can be." Katherine placed her elbows on the wooden table. "But we aren't restricted to such timelines like others are."

I heard the two guys across from us stand, and I turned in Dreamy's direction. Damn, he was built. I hadn't noticed how broad his shoulders were until he stood, and his loose t-shirt clung to each one of his muscles. He had to be over six feet tall, which meant he would tower over me. I'd never seen a human that large without the help of steroids. But there wasn't a toxic fume surrounding him, so it was all authentic and him.

His gaze met mine, and the world seemed to stop.

He paused, and for a second, I thought he was coming over.

The corner of his friend's mouth tipped upward. "You okay, man?"

"Yeah, I'm fine," he said in a deep, husky voice.

His words made me feel raw ... naked. Hell, they almost felt like a caress on my skin.

"Then why aren't you moving?" His friend's voice shook with laughter.

The guy tore his eyes from mine and glared at his best friend. "I am." He took a few steps toward the boys' dorm.

"Oh, hey." The guy's friend stopped beside me. "You deserve better than that asshole."

He was being nice, but I was so damn tired of everyone telling me what I needed or deserved. "How do you know that? Maybe I'm a bitch."

Roxy's mouth dropped so low it almost hit the table. *Sadie!*

"Yeah ..." Dreamy's friend huffed and shook his head. "Sure sounds like you are."

Dreamy grabbed his friend's arm and tugged him away. "Just come on." Disappointment flashed across his face.

For some reason, that hurt worse than my father's disappointment, which was saying something. *I'm an asshole.* I wished I could take back the words.

Our table remained silent until the guys were out of human hearing distance. They were the only two who'd been at risk of overhearing our conversation.

"See." Dreamy leaned into his friend. "That's why we aren't nice to anyone."

And I'd already given him a poor impression of me. Just great.

"Color me surprised." Lillith turned so her side leaned against the table. "How much bite do you have in there, little pup?"

And the dog jokes had officially started.

"I'm just as shocked." Roxy tilted her head, examining me. "She's normally not confrontational like that."

"Oh, stop it." I felt like a complete ass, and them going on about it was only making it worse. "I don't know what came over me."

"It's good to play hard to get." Katherine winked. "You don't want to come off too interested."

"I wasn't interested in him." I had my eye set on the friend, but that didn't matter. "Besides, it's for the best. My dad would flip if I intermingled with humans."

"If that asshole alpha would calm his shit down, it wouldn't be nearly as huge of a deal." Lillith stiffened with anger. "I mean, he even considers half, if not more of our kind to be too weak, so what's the big deal? Some humans make a better lay."

My dad's stance was renowned throughout the supernatural community. He boasted that most people, even outside the shifter race, viewed him as a leader. It was true because he didn't have a problem with blackmailing, bribing, or killing to stay on top.

"Oh my God." Roxy turned toward Lillith. "How do you know that?"

"Let's just say our nest pretends to go along with the masses, but we like to go out on a limb from time to time and keep to ourselves." Lillith twirled her hair with her finger. "And I've had the privilege of sleeping with a human man or two."

"Lillith." Katherine lifted a hand. "You need to be careful who you tell these things to. You never know ..."

"Oh, please." Lillith waved her off. "These two are way too nice to be associated with that asshole's pack."

Roxy snorted before clamping a hand over her mouth.

"Wait ..." Lillith glanced from her to me. "Are you from Tyler's pack?"

I wanted to lie, but they deserved to know the truth. "Yeah ..."

"Not only are we from his pack, but ..." Roxy lifted a finger and swirled it in my direction. "... she's the alpha heir."

"See." Katherine lowered her chest to the table. "Now look what you've done. Our asses are toast."

"No, they aren't." They thought I would run and tell him. "I came here to get away from them. Your secret is safe with us."

"I do have a question, though." Roxy chewed on her bottom lip. "How are you two out in the sun? I thought ..."

"That we're cursed to a life in darkness?" Katherine curled her fingers and inspected her pale pink nails. "No, we haven't succumbed to our dark urges."

It was comforting that they hadn't. Most of the vampires we'd dealt with didn't mind getting their hands dirty. When vampires gave up their humanity, it became harder for them to be in sunlight. If they kept their humanity, they were essentially human but with a super-long life and blood cravings. My father wouldn't want me associating with Katherine and Lillith because they weren't the strongest of their kind. In his eyes, they couldn't do what needed to be done.

"Being a vampire sounds perfect." Roxy patted the area around her eyes. "Never having to worry about crow's feet."

"You still have a longer life than humans do." Shifters could easily live up to two hundred years. We even had a few who'd reached two hundred and fifty.

"True." Roxy bobbed her head. "But not infinite."

"Just remember; when you're two hundred and all

wrinkly"—Lillith motioned to her face—"I'll still be looking like this."

"You bitch," Roxy growled good-naturedly.

"It's not easy being a vampire." Katherine tapped her fingers on the table. "Your instincts are to kill and be vile. You fight them every day to keep your humanity. The ones who lose their humanity either wanted to be a vampire or lost someone they loved and turned off the pain."

"Oh wow." I hadn't thought about outliving all of my loved ones. It had to be a nightmare. "That would suck."

"Are you trying to be funny?" Lillith chuckled. "Or was that unintentional?"

I had to be missing something. "What do you mean?"

She pressed her thumb to her incisor. "It would suck to be a vampire?"

"No. Sorry." Being around these two wasn't nearly as strange as I'd expected. Dad made it sound like all of us supernaturals were so different from one another, but we really weren't. We were four girls looking for a chance at a normal life.

My ALARM BLARED, startling me awake. I had my very first calculus class at nine, and choosing such an early class already felt like a bad idea.

Roxy threw the pillow on top of her face. "I can't believe you talked me into this blasphemy."

She had told me it was too damn early, but I'd convinced her to take the class with me, anyway. "Oh, stop." I yawned as I said, "It's not that bad."

"I'm sorry." She lifted the side of the pillow so I could

see her scowling face. "I couldn't understand you through that huge-ass yawn."

I threw the covers off me and placed my feet on the fuzzy beige carpet. "Bite me."

"Those vampires sure did you in," she said as she stretched. "You've been all about sucking and biting here lately."

"Maybe we shouldn't hang out with them anymore." After we'd finished our little chat outside, the vampires had helped Roxy and me set up our room. The look on Brock's face when he'd come to get me for dinner had almost had me bursting out in a peal of laughter. "You and Lillith could almost be twins."

"I couldn't pull off her look." She fluffed her hair. "This red wouldn't allow me to achieve the dark, gothic look."

"You could always dye it." She never would. She was proud of her bright red hair that wasn't common in the shifter world. Apparently, that's how she'd known we were meant to be besties. Our colorful hair set us apart from the rest.

Brock had informed me that his first class wasn't until noon and that he would be sleeping in and that I should call him if something happened. I wouldn't call him if a clown with an axe showed up at my door. I'd rather die a slow, tragic death than subject myself to him more than I had to. "Let's get up and grab something to eat."

Just as I'd expected, she sat upright. "You do know the right words to say to me."

We ran to the dorm bathroom and quickly showered and got dressed. Once we'd fixed our hair and makeup, we were ready to take on the day.

We entered the Student Center and walked past the circle of couches right in the doorway and toward the open area where at least twenty booths lined the walls and fifty square tables were arranged in rows. In a few sections, students pushed the tables together so a bigger group could sit with each other.

"For it being this early, it's pretty crowded." There were still a few open tables sporadically spaced throughout the room. "We better hurry or we might not be able to find a vacant table."

The scent of bacon overwhelmed my senses. We went over to a breakfast station where biscuits were individually wrapped and ready to go.

As I reached for one, my body collided with a brick wall. I bounced off it and almost fell on my ass, but strong, warm hands gripped my shoulders. Then, an all-too-familiar sexy voice rasped, "Watch where you're going."

It took a second for it to sink in. The hot guy from yesterday had his hands on me, but he glared at me with such disdain.

CHAPTER THREE

His hands stayed on my shoulders, which surprised me. I'd expected him to drop his hands with repulsion. My heart sped up from his proximity.

He acted annoyed but continued touching me, which gave me mixed signals. I wasn't interested in whatever game he wanted to play. I lifted my chin and channeled all of my rage toward him. "Maybe you should watch where you're going?"

The room quieted, and all I could hear was his rapid breathing. He rasped, "I was already here."

I should have moved out of his grasp, but my legs wouldn't allow it. Even though his fingers dug gently into my skin, it made butterflies take flight in my stomach. I didn't understand what was going on between us.

Finally, he dropped his hands to his sides, but then he took a step closer to me. In the next moment, it sounded like he took a sniff of my hair. I was most likely losing my damn mind.

I needed to end this encounter, but of course, that wasn't what I did.

He reached around me and grabbed the very biscuit we'd both been aiming for. "Better luck next time." He waved it in front of my face, gloating like a jackass.

In a flash, I snatched the biscuit from him. The way he blinked several times in shock almost had me keeling over in laughter.

To gloat, I took a bite and chewed with my mouth wide open. "This has got to be the best damn biscuit I've ever had."

Roxy snorted and took a biscuit for herself. "Come on, Sadie. Let's go find a seat." She pulled me away, but I couldn't tear my gaze from him.

"Uh ..." His friend took two biscuits from the bar. "I found you a replacement." A shit-eating smirk filled his face. "Unless you wanna go chase her down and finish off that one? But with how she's chowing down, I bet it's almost gone."

The thought of him following through on his friend's suggestion thrilled me. Whatever was going on between us was not normal or healthy.

"Shut up," Dreamy said as he took a biscuit from his friend and headed to the cash register. I didn't need him catching me watching him.

Roxy paid the cashier and headed toward the tables. "Are you proud of yourself?"

"Hey." My shoulders were still warm from his touch. "He was being an ass. I merely stood up for myself."

"You know I approve of that." She walked over to a booth next to a large group of humans. "But the sexual tension was thick."

"What?" My voice rose to dangerously high levels. "It was not."

"I think you protest a little too much, and let's be real,

even a dead wolf could smell it." Roxy chuckled as she slid into one side of the booth and motioned for me to sit across from her. "I mean, he is hot."

And human. I linked with her, not wanting prying ears to overhear. I doubted anyone was listening, but we couldn't be too careful. "I'm not here to meet a man. I'm here to have fun and get an education."

"You know, that goes along with fun." Roxy stuck a straw in her orange juice and moved it in and out suggestively, then took a big swig. "Just like vodka should always be part of orange juice."

I refused to laugh at her. I took a large sip of my hot coffee instead, letting it burn on the way down. I squirmed with discomfort. "Vodka doesn't even get you drunk." Every shifter needed wolfsbane or to chug straight liquor to get them there. We had a fast metabolism, so the wolfsbane slowed down our ability to quickly process alcohol.

"Hey, I'm dedicated to the cause." She unwrapped her biscuit and sniffed. "Just like I'm dedicated to getting this in my belly."

A giggle escaped despite my best efforts. "If I hadn't gone to high school with you, I might not realize how smart you actually are." She was basically a genius. Well ... okay, that was an exaggeration, but she'd made A's and B's throughout school without trying.

She stuffed her mouth. "Says the valedictorian."

"Sexy." Watching her chew her food turned my stomach. "Real sexy."

"Oh." She opened her mouth wider. "I thought after what you did to that guy, you enjoyed eating like this."

"Me." I patted my chest. "Not you."

"Pfft." She shoved the biscuit into her mouth, letting crumbs fall all over the table.

"If you're not careful, I'll get the last laugh," I said and took another bite, eating like a lady should.

She tried speaking around a huge mouthful of food. "Hww ... sho?"

"You're already over halfway done eating your biscuit." I lifted my hand, emphasizing my barely eaten food. "And I have more left to eat than you. You'll be wanting some of mine, and I'm not sharing."

"You bish," she choked and grabbed her juice, sucking it down.

"Aw, you love me." We'd given each other shit for as long as I could remember. "Your ramblings don't scare me."

She wrinkled her nose. "Don't be so sure."

Some kids at the table next to us stood, and one of the girls sighed. "I guess we better head to class."

Roxy grumbled. "Shit, how did the time go by so fast?" She threw her empty wrapper on the tray. "And to think you thought you'd have the last laugh. I'm done eating, and you're not."

"No biggie." I stood, slid my purple backpack over my shoulder, and grabbed my food and coffee. "I can multitask, unlike some people."

"The one time I fell while walking wasn't due to me chewing gum." She picked up her tray and carried it to the garbage. "That bitch Kelly started that rumor."

I tsked and followed her. "I'm not so sure."

She stuck her tongue out at me. "Oh, bite me."

I normally didn't goad her like this. She usually did it to me. "Now who's the one obsessed with the vampires?"

She turned toward me and feigned shock. "Who are you?"

"Stop it." Maybe this semester wouldn't be so bad after all. "We'd better hurry."

"Don't act so smug." She adjusted her mustard shirt over her dark gray slacks. "I'll get my revenge."

We rushed out of the Student Center and headed to the right, passing the sidewalk that led to Kortright Stadium and staying on the path of the large circle, moving straight to Wilson Hall for Calculus. Grey Hall was on the other side of the grassy area, directly across from the Student Center, with Webster Hall to the left and Wilson Hall to the right.

Four small brownstone steps led up to the dark wood double doors. This particular building was three stories high, and in the middle, above the doorway, the roof stood higher than the rest of the building as if it had once been a bell tower.

I pulled the schedule out of my pocket. "We're on the first floor."

We entered the building and quickly found our room.

When we walked in, I scanned the classroom. There were four rows of seats and no windows as the classroom was in the middle of the building. A familiar dark-haired vampire sat at the very back of the third row.

She gave us a little wave, but even from here, I could see how tired she was.

I usually liked sitting at the front, but humans already filled the desks in the front section. "Let's head back there."

No one sat near her; humans' natural instincts told them to stay away from Lillith. Even though vampires were attractive, humans felt self-conscious around them. They likely felt like prey even if they didn't understand it.

Roxy went down the second row and sat at the open desk beside our friend. "You must stink or something," Roxy said as she nodded to the humans who sat as far away from her as possible. "Maybe showering would help."

"I'd normally be ready to banter, but Katherine kept me

up last night." Lillith placed her arms on her desk and lowered her head. "She was giggling and talking about how we'd finally made it."

"Made it?" I asked as I passed by a handsome blond man who turned his head to follow my movement. I sat right in front of the vampire. "What does that mean?" The guy was cute, but he didn't even tempt me. Not like Dreamy.

God ... I had to stop calling him that. It was downright ridiculous even if it was true.

"Yeah, our ... parents aren't keen on us going to school." Lillith lifted her head and glowered at the human still staring at us. "Why don't you just bugger off?"

"Uh ..." The guy's mouth opened and closed. "Sorry." He turned around, facing the front.

"Bugger off?" Roxy's shoulders shook. "What are you? English?"

"Actually, I hail from London." She rubbed her eyes. "It was just so damn long ago."

That little nugget of information hit me hard. I'd assumed they were our age, but they could be hundreds of years old, for all we knew. "How long ago was that?" I probably shouldn't have asked the question here, but I was dying to know.

She lowered her voice so only Roxy and I could hear. "I left there two hundred years ago, but that's a story for another time."

Of course, that's when the professor decided to walk in and begin class.

I split from Lillith and Roxy, walking toward Grey Hall for English. Lillith had some sort of science class while Roxy was heading to the gym for a weight class. She'd kept harping on about how she hoped she had some eye candy while working out. She'd gotten annoyed when I'd reminded her to make sure she didn't stick out like a sore thumb. We needed to keep a low profile and not raise any questions.

This building was a little more modern than Wilson Hall, but not by much. It was a standard, two-story brick building, and my class happened to be on the top floor. The entryway was flat, and I opened the large single door and walked inside. A single stairway sat to the immediate right before the main entrance to the first floor.

People passed me as I walked up the stairway. The steps were narrow and barely large enough for two people to pass each other comfortably. When I got to the top floor, I followed the room numbers until I found my classroom.

I walked in, and my heart dropped. This room was smaller with only three rows of desks. Of course, Dreamy's friend would be in here with me. He sat at the very back, and the only open seat was situated between him and another guy.

He glared at me as he tapped his pen hard on his binder, causing his blue shirt to bunch with each motion. He crossed his ankles, which brought my attention to his worn, holey jeans.

For a split second, I considered walking out and missing class, but I couldn't let someone dictate my life any more than I already was. I tugged at my wolf, hoping to gain some confidence from her. I sucked in a breath, and the faint scent of fire hit my nose.

My eyes landed on a large man sitting at the back. He'd

have looked awkwardly huge in that desk if he hadn't been sexy as sin. His long, honey-blond hair was styled upward, and sandy blond scruff covered his chin. He wore a polo shirt that hugged him like a second skin. His dragon bled through as the pupils in his golden eyes changed to slits before evening back out to the round human-shaped ones.

Dragons were super rare, but this university attracted supernaturals of all kinds. I didn't know anyone who'd ever met a dragon. Their kind was almost extinct due to humans hunting them down. Roxy would be so damn jealous. I had a feeling she'd be stalking my classroom just to steal a peek.

I stupidly decided to take the seat between Dragon Man and Dreamy's friend. I squeezed past the humans, and the friend was already openly scowling at me.

Trying to push my discomfort away, I sat in my seat, unzipped my bag, and pulled out my binder and English book.

The dragon turned in my direction but didn't say a word.

Picking up my pen, I rolled it across my binder. I stared at the paper, acting like I saw the most interesting thing in the entire world even though it was blank.

"Do you have an extra pen?" the dragon guy asked. His voice held a slight accent that I'd never heard before.

"Uh ... yeah." I grabbed a black pen and handed it to him. "Keep it. I've got plenty."

"Thanks." He smiled as he held my gaze. He was most likely trying to figure out what I was.

"No problem."

"I'm Egan," he said as he held out a hand.

"Sadie." I gave him a small smile as I placed my hand in his. It looked tiny compared to his.

"Nice to meet you." I could feel the strong animal just underneath his skin.

"You're only nice to playboy-looking guys?" the friend asked beside me. "Figures. I regret being nice to you."

The fact that he was talking to me like this shocked me. "It was rude of you to assume something when you know nothing about me." I kept my voice leveled so as not to reveal my annoyance. I had been an ass, but he was giving it right back to me.

"Yes, it was so offensive that I thought you didn't deserve to have a controlling boyfriend who was manhandling you in front of everyone." The guy's brown eyes narrowed, and that was when I noticed he was actually quite large for a human himself.

"First off, he's not my boyfriend." I didn't know why I'd felt like I should clarify. Actually, I did. I didn't want Dreamy to think I was taken, but I didn't want to admit it. "And secondly, even if you meant well, it was none of your damn business."

"Yeah ..." The guy crossed his arms. "I got that, and don't worry. We won't make that mistake again."

He couldn't mean ... "We?"

"My boy, Donovan." He winced and shook his head. "You were a bitch to him this morning in the cafeteria."

He had to be kidding, surely. "He ran into me." I didn't even notice him standing there.

"Oh ... I get it now." The guy hit his binder with his hand. "You're one of those victims, right? No matter what life throws at you, it's not your fault."

I was getting pissed, and my wolf was about to bleed through. "What does that even mean?"

"Don't let him get you riled up." Egan touched my arm.

"His type likes to find fault in everyone. It makes it easier for them."

"My type?" The guy huffed. "What do you mean by that?"

Egan responded quickly, "The broken and hard."

"Welcome to Composition 101," the professor said as he breezed into the classroom. "Let's begin class."

However, the two of them didn't seem to hear him as they stared each other down.

CHAPTER FOUR

The one good thing I'd learned in this class was that *his* name was Donovan and the friend was Axel. The bad thing was that Egan and Axel had glared at each other throughout the entire class.

And I thought women held grudges. Figured that was another old wives' tale made up by arrogant, self-centered men.

As class wrapped up, I got my things together and placed them in my backpack. As soon as we were allowed to leave, I'd cut my losses and get out of here as quickly as possible. Those two could have it out without me.

I probably should have been more worried since Axel was human, but I found my ability to care lacking even though I wasn't sure what that said about me.

Right when I had the green light to go, I jumped to my feet and shuffled behind the four people in front of me to the door.

I tried not crowding the humans, but it was so damn hard. My escape mode was fully activated.

As I stepped into the hallway, I almost jumped with joy, but Egan called out, "Hey, Sadie."

Apparently, he was more interested in talking to me than eating Axel for a snack. That sucked.

I glanced over my shoulder, only slowing my pace marginally. He was a dragon, so he could keep up. "Yeah?"

He sped up and caught up to me in seconds. "You were eager to get out of class."

I bounded down the stairs. "Don't want to be late for my next one."

That wasn't a lie, so he couldn't call me out on it. Shifters in general were keen on smells and what they meant. Our sense of smell was similar to the way we super-naturals could hear the changes in heart rate too. No matter the senses we used, it was easy to detect a lie even from several hundred feet away.

"So was that ..." He stopped himself, keeping close behind me. "... person sitting next to you in class the reason for you rushing out?"

Of course, he'd be smart and ask the right question. The rumor was that dragons were very intelligent. "Maybe."

I sounded weak for letting a human affect me like that. Even though our supernatural population was large, the human one was three times larger. If they found out about us, we'd risk the danger of becoming used for experiments and God knew what. I had an irrational fear that they might even create a zoo for supernaturals.

I hit the bottom floor and headed out the double doors.

"But why?" he asked, walking beside me. His intense gaze penetrated my defenses, making me want to stop in place. However, this wasn't a conversation we could have out in the open like this.

"Because that's how things work." It wasn't like I could

give him a clear answer right now. "If you're here, you should know this."

If he didn't realize he had to keep a large distance between him and humans, it was important for him to know the truth. He seemed like a good guy, and I'd hate for something to happen to him.

"Yeah ... I'm figuring out there's a lot we don't know." He scanned the people walking by us. "Can we go out to dinner or something?"

I stopped in my tracks. "Are you asking me out on a date?"

"What? No." He shook his head and cringed. "Not that you aren't intriguing or gorgeous." His brows furrowed. "I ..."

"Hey, no." His odd discomfort made me feel a million times better. I had a hard time relating to others, mainly because the way my dad treated me made me feel like I didn't know how to act and was a complete and utter embarrassment. It was difficult to overcome those feeling but was something I planned to work on while I was here. "It's fine. You just caught me off guard."

My dad would be ecstatic if I snagged a dragon, which meant I wouldn't date him even if I wanted to.

He scratched the back of his neck. "So ..."

"Sure." Brock would be thrilled. It would be another thing he could boast about: meeting a rare dragon. "I'd like to invite a few more people if that's cool."

"People like us?" he asked with hope.

"Yes, there are more than just us here. I do need to get to my next class, but how about we meet at the Student Center at six?"

"Yeah, that sounds great." He turned toward Wilson Hall. "See you soon."

I watched him for a second. The guy was fucking huge. He had to be over seven feet tall, given the way he towered over everyone.

As girls passed him, they would do a double-take. I had a feeling this poor guy didn't have a clue what he was getting himself into.

Forcing myself to head to class, I picked up my pace. I fought to keep myself from walking too fast because it was a beautiful morning, and I felt energized.

Webster Hall was an all-brick building like the others, and it was a little larger, likely due to the labs associated with the science classes. It was a four-story building with a slanted roof, probably built between the time Wilson Hall and Grey Hall were constructed. It seemed to have been in the architectural style of buildings between those two eras.

The double wooden doors leading into the building were on the ground level, and more people were heading into this building than the others. I had Psychology 101 here, and it was on the top floor.

There were stairs in between the inner and outer entrances, similar to the other buildings. I went to the right, avoiding the mass of students heading out the doors.

Two girls were walking in front of me very slowly and laughing about something. I didn't care enough to listen to what it might be. I just wanted them to move. They continued up the stairs after the second floor, and my patience wore thin.

I rubbed my hands along my jean shorts to calm my nerves. I'd have to get used to dealing with human slowness. Most of the students here were human, so it was par for the course.

They exited onto the third floor, and I blew out a breath. Finally, I could move at a faster pace.

On the top floor, I hurried, looking for the classroom. The crowd in the hallways was thinning as students scattered to the classrooms, which meant that the number of available seats would be slim pickings.

I stepped into the classroom, and his scent filled my nose. I felt as if a magnet was pulling me toward him. I spotted Donovan sitting at the very back just like his friend. I was the last person in the class. Stupid slow humans.

The seat in front of Donovan was the only one available out of twenty. Dammit, that would be my luck. After this morning, I wasn't sure whether to expect another round of confrontation or if I should prepare to be ignored.

It didn't matter. I'd face this head-on. I straightened my shoulders and slid between two people to get to my seat. I dropped my bag on the floor and sat in my chair.

My heart raced, but I didn't smell any supernaturals, so no one would be alerted to my discomfort.

"Hey." The guy beside me saluted, causing his black shirt to wrinkle around his shoulder. "Are you new here?" His green eyes twinkled as he leaned toward me.

His buddies beside him chuckled. One of them leaned over and whispered to another guy, "He wants to bang the most girls this semester. Look at him jump on her."

"She's hot." The other one glanced my way. "I don't blame him one bit."

Great, this dude wanted to make me another notch on his bedpost. Classy. I needed to shut this down now. "Not interested."

"I'm a sophomore this year." He grinned at me and ran his fingers through his short beard. "And I figured psychology class would be a good investment. That way, I can be the best husband possible, emotionally, for my future wife."

This guy smelled like rotten eggs, revealing his lie. "Once again, not interested."

"I'm not so sure that's a true statement about being emotionally available for your wife," Donovan said lowly behind me. "You seem more like the douche-player kind. A class like this won't knock the trash out of you."

A snort escaped me before I even registered that it was leaving.

"Besides ..." I felt Donovan's gaze land on me without turning around. "... this one is taken."

"Sorry, man." The guy lifted his hands. "I didn't realize she was your girl."

"She's not." He shook his head hard, and his nose wrinkled in disgust. "I don't like being saddled down."

I turned around in my seat and narrowed my eyes at him. "What is your problem?"

"Damn," one of the douche's friends muttered. "She's scary."

Donovan leaned back in his chair and placed his arms behind his head. "It's nothing personal. I don't date anyone even if they're hot." A hint of arousal billowed off him.

I wasn't sure if he was complimenting me. And I wondered if I was mistaken about his scent. He acted like I grossed him out, and the fact that he was getting under my skin pissed me off. "I'm thinking it's due to your self-loathing. You like to project it on everyone else."

"You think I hate myself?" He grinned smugly and looked unimpressed. "That's the most unoriginal line I've ever heard."

He brought out the worst in me, and I didn't know why. But I'd be damned if I would sit here and let him talk down to me. "It's a good thing I'm not worried about impressing you, then." My wolf surged forward, and I fisted my hands, allowing my nails to cut into my palms. I had to end this before I lost control.

It was for mere survival that I faced the front again. Everything inside me told me to have it out with him, and then naughty thoughts entered my head—like the way he would look without those clothes. I had to stop my thoughts from going any further.

I THOUGHT the class would never end. As it progressed, Donovan's scent grew stronger, and I felt his breath hit the back of my neck. The bastard must have been leaning over his desk.

As soon as the professor began talking about the next class, I packed up my stuff and sat on the edge of my seat. I was ready to get out of here and now.

Within seconds of the professor's dismissal, I stood and forced myself not to shove by all of the other students. I needed distance from Donovan and fast. My phone buzzed in my pocket, and I pulled it out as I hit the hallway.

Meet us at the Student Center, Hussy.

I'd told Roxy not to call me that name a hundred times, but it only made her call me that more. If I didn't love her to death, I'd hate the bitch.

With the vague "us," I was assuming she didn't mean Brock. I glanced at the time and saw that it was eleven fifty, so we should be safe. His classes began at noon. Maybe I'd actually get a reprieve for most of the day.

He was also on the football team, so that was a win for me as well. He'd have late afternoon practices and games on the weekends.

In the Student Center, I found Roxy, Katherine, and

Lillith sitting together at a booth. The seat beside Roxy was vacant, so I headed over and put my stuff down.

Both vampires had coffee cups, but a strong metallic smell came from them. They were hiding their blood.

"I'm going to grab a burger and fries," I said and dug out my wallet from my bag. A steak would've been ideal, but beggars couldn't be choosers here.

"Oh ... will you get me one too?" Roxy rubbed her stomach. "I'm hungry and rushed here to get a table."

"Sure." It was only fair. She'd bought me breakfast this morning.

I hurried into the cafeteria and found Axel and Donovan there together.

No matter where I went, those two assholes showed up. Out of everyone in the entire school, two out of three classes, so far, had one of them in it. Hadn't I endured enough?

They were standing across the room, so all should be well. I headed into the cafeteria on the other side and made a beeline straight to the burger line. I looked for them.

My heart calmed slightly when I didn't notice them in the cafeteria. Maybe I'd get by this time without an awkward confrontation.

I pulled my phone out and scrolled through friends' updates. Most of the pack members didn't leave for college like I did, so there were just a lot of pictures of them hiking and whatnot. Nothing that would appear too strange for human eyes.

When I was almost at the front of the line, the all too appealing smell hit my nose. Dammit, they were heading this way. However, if I went back to Roxy without food, I'd never hear the end of it. She was already teasing me; I didn't need to push it and make her suspicious. She'd never let it go, and I had a feeling my new vampy friends wouldn't either.

Donovan got in line a few people behind me.

The smart thing to do would be to keep my eyes forward and not engage, but I quickly learned I was, in fact, not a smart person. We had a class together, so playing nice would be in my favor. "Don't even try to claim I stole your food this time," I said teasingly.

He *hmphed* and licked his bottom lip, but he didn't respond. Instead, he focused on the menu above the grill.

Well, he'd made it clear that he didn't want to talk to me. Great.

The two guys between us stared awkwardly at the ground.

Yeah, I didn't blame them. I'd be doing the same thing.

"Dude." Axel walked over, oblivious to my presence. "I thought you were getting pizza. You talked about it the entire way here." He paused and followed Donovan's gaze right to me.

CHAPTER FIVE

"**R**eally?" Axel sighed. "Of course you'd want a burger now."

My heart warmed even though it shouldn't have. If he'd come over here because of me, then he was struggling with the same damn feelings.

"Shut up." Donovan glared, his jaw set. "I want both."

Axel lowered his voice. "Because we have that kind of cash?"

He'd said it quietly, so he didn't think I'd heard, but with my hearing, he might as well have said it in his normal voice.

"I told you, I'm going to look for a job tonight." Donovan avoided looking at his friend. "Everything will be fine."

"I sure hope you're right." Axel cracked his neck. "I'll grab us a table." He turned and made his way to the registers.

"What kind of burger do you want?" the cook asked, getting my attention.

My stomach rumbled. "Two double bacon burgers, please. Medium-rare."

The older man put four patties on the grill. "Uh ... are you sure you want medium-rare? It might make you sick."

"Positive." It shocked me how humans wanted their meat fully cooked. It lost all its flavor when it was cooked through.

"Okay." He grabbed four buns, coated them with butter, and put them on the grill. He then pulled some already cooked bacon out of a tin tub.

He took the next few people's orders while I stood there, playing on my phone again. I needed a distraction so I wouldn't be tempted to look at him.

After Donovan placed his order, he stood closer to me. His scent overshadowed the smell of the delicious, greasy meat.

I glanced at him out of the corner of my eye, and his head jerked forward.

He was stealing glances at me, and it should have terrified me, not thrilled me.

He bounced his leg and ran his hands through his hair. He nibbled on his lip, and his face softened as he faced me. "Two double burgers, huh? Want to become a fat-ass?"

His words took a second to register. He'd been a growly ass to me, but this was a cheap shot, especially since it had looked like he was going to be nice. "Well, you keep stalking me, so I have to figure out a way to get you to leave me the hell alone."

The fact that he'd hurt me made this attraction even worse because I still wasn't repelled by him. I mean, what did that say about me? I refused to have a mate who treated me the way my father did. Why was I even using the word *mate* when referencing him? I wanted to face-palm myself for the thought.

Needing space, I grabbed the plate with both burgers and stepped toward the cashiers.

"Don't flatter yourself." Donovan straightened his back. "There's only one place to eat on campus, and it's lunchtime."

"Maybe you should've gotten your pizza first, then." I marched away from him, keeping my head straight and refusing to cower.

When I made it back to the girls, Roxy lifted an eyebrow and asked, "Is everything okay?"

"Yeah." I slipped onto the seat next to her and placed the plate between us. "Just starving."

"Your heart is racing a mile a minute." Lillith took a huge swig of her blood. "If that doesn't prove you're lying, I'll dress up in rainbow colors tomorrow and pretend to be a unicorn."

"Oh ... and poop out rainbows." Roxy grinned and nodded. "While carrying around four puppies."

"Stop getting excited," Lillith said, shooting Roxy a go-to-hell look. "She's obviously lying, so this won't actually be a thing."

"Uh ..." Roxy jerked her head from side to side. "She's not lying."

The air around us smelled like rotten eggs.

"Oh God." Katherine rubbed her forehead. "Everyone, just stop. Obviously, Sadie lied, but she doesn't want to talk about it, so we're going to be good friends and let it go."

"Wait." Roxy frowned. "I never agreed to that. Letting it go doesn't make you a good friend."

"I don't know." I had to give her shit—anything to get

the attention off me. "You do always force yourself on me. Maybe she has a point."

"Please." Roxy flipped her hair over her shoulder and grabbed the burger. "You know you love me."

I SPENT the rest of the afternoon in my dorm room, working on my homework. I needed to get a head start on my classes. Dad had made a point to tell me if my scholarship fell through, I'd be coming home. He'd almost sounded like he hoped I'd fail. Just another thing for him to hold against me to prove I was an embarrassment.

A loud knock sounded on the door, startling me from my psychology reading.

Let me guess. Roxy lifted her head from her pillow and glared at the door. *Satan is here.*

Don't insult Satan like that. I'd hoped that football practice would run over and keep Brock from making dinner. *He has more redeeming qualities than that jackass.*

True. Roxy tossed her phone aside and stood. *You're making me answer the door, which is cruel.*

You're watching videos while I'm trying to finish this chapter. I swore I'd read the same line at least five times. *It'll just take a second.*

She opened the door and waved her hand in front of her face. "Dude, you stink."

The overly strong musky scent floated into the room. He needed to lay off whatever cologne he used.

"I do not." He rolled his eyes. "I showered at the gym after practice. Are you both ready?"

There went any chance of me finishing this. I stood and

glanced at the time. It was five minutes to six. "Yeah, we need to get over there. Egan should be there any second."

"Egan?" Brock tilted his head and scowled. "Who the hell is that?"

"Oh ..." Roxy clapped her hands and ran them down her dress, smoothing it down. "A dragon shifter."

"What?" He rubbed a finger along his lip. "You're joking, right?"

"Nope." It'd been at least fifty years since anyone had seen a dragon or, at least, that I knew of. "I couldn't believe it myself. He doesn't seem to know the supernaturals' ways or laws, so I thought we could help him out."

"Definitely." Brock smirked. "Dragons are fierce allies, so good job. Your dad would be proud."

That wasn't what mattered to me. I sincerely only wanted to help him out. Of course, Brock would think about it in terms of power and prestige. I merely thought it had been cool to meet one.

"Let's not keep the man waiting." Roxy waggled her brows at me. *He is sexy, right? At least, I'll have some eye candy, unlike this morning.*

She'd been pouting all day that the gym had shut down for her class, so there had been no one else in there except for the ladies working out.

Yes, he is handsome. Which was strange since he'd had no effect on me whatsoever. *You'll enjoy yourself.*

The three of us headed to the Student Center. It wasn't hard to spot Egan. He towered over everyone, and a few girls surrounded him, trying to catch his attention.

He must have smelled us because his head turned in our direction, and his attention landed right on me. A small smile lit up his face.

Roxy grabbed my arm. *Holy shit. You didn't tell me he looks like a fucking god.*

Leave it up to her to be all dramatic. *Gods don't exist.* I tried not to laugh.

She bumped into me. *You know what I mean.*

"Sadie," he said in his low voice. "I see you followed through on your promise to bring friends." He walked over to us, and the girls pouted.

"Yes." Humans could be so ridiculous sometimes. "This is my best friend, Roxy, and ..." I wasn't sure what to call Brock. "... an ally, Brock."

"Ally?" Egan pursed his lips and held his hand out to Brock. "I'm Egan."

"Nice to meet you." Brock shook hands with him eagerly. "Sadie told me all about you on the way over here."

It was crazy that Egan towered over Brock. As a future alpha, Brock was one of the tallest shifters.

"All about me?" Egan chuckled and pointed at me. "I didn't realize we'd gotten so acquainted."

"He's exaggerating." I didn't need Egan to think I wanted something from him. "I pretty much told them what you are and how it would be nice to have you as a friend."

"A friend." Egan turned to Roxy and shook her hand as well. "I like the sound of that. I don't have too many of those back home."

"Speaking of home," Brock began, jumping right to the point, "where is that, exactly?"

"Not trying to be rude, but I'm not at liberty to say." He surveyed the area around us and motioned to the humans. "It's sort of a secret, for reasons I'm sure you know."

I understood his meaning. Humans had almost wiped out dragons. "No worries at all." I pointed to the doors.

"Why don't we grab some food and eat somewhere outside, away from eavesdroppers."

"Now that sounds like a good idea." Roxy gestured to the gym. "Some tables over there should be vacant. They're near the woods too. Some of the humans were complaining about the bugs, so we could have a decent shot of being alone."

Our group split once we got into the cafeteria. Roxy and I grabbed some chicken parmesan and headed outside to wait on the group.

If I'd thought wolf shifters ate a ton, I now stood corrected.

Egan held a tray in each hand, and they were filled with food such as pizza, wings, burgers, and pasta. Pretty much, if you named it, it could be found there.

There was no way he could eat it all. "Got enough?"

"I was worried about that too." He grimaced and scanned his food. "Should I go back and get some more?"

Roxy lifted a hand. "You didn't get dessert."

"Holy shit." His eyes widened. "You're right. I knew I liked you for a reason."

She giggled. *He likes me.*

Maybe you've found your shifter for all the fun things you have planned. Sometimes, I worried about her.

That sobered her up. *Yeah ... Lord knows I'm not strong enough to date a dragon shifter.*

Hey. I hated that we had to worry about stupid shit like that. If people liked each other, they should be able to date. *If the dragon chooses to date you, it's on him.*

Egan glided toward the library. "I'll go back for dessert later."

The fact was, *gliding* wasn't an exaggeration. The food on his tray didn't even rattle with his grace. If I tried doing that, I'd trip over my feet, and my pasta would be on top of my head. Envy didn't even touch how I felt.

Brock, Roxy, and I marched after him.

Behind the huge modern library and gym was a small open area with two wooden picnic tables right next to the woods. The tree line was thick, and the branches stretched out across the clearing, shading it from the sun.

As Roxy had expected, no one was out here. Snakes had to be close by because I clearly heard the rattles.

Brock and Egan sat on one side while Roxy and I sat on the other.

As expected, Brock dove right back into his line of questioning. "Now that we're away from humans, where does the rest of your clan live?"

Egan took a large bite of his all-meat pizza and chewed slowly. "Because of our dwindling population, we don't share our location with anyone outside our kind."

"But we're shifters." Brock forced a laugh. "We can trust one another."

I wanted to tell Egan, "Don't. Don't trust us." My dad and Brock's pack would use anything they could to stay in complete control. The dragons were fierce warriors and the biggest threat to wolves retaining the most control.

"I'm sure that's true," Egan said as his dragon-shaped pupils landed back on me. I shook my head ever so slightly, hoping he picked up on my nonverbal message.

His pupils went back to their normal shape. "But I'd be going against my family's wishes, so I can't. I'm sure you understand."

Thank God. "I can respect that," I chimed in to defuse any more of Brock's attempts to get that information.

Brock frowned. "So, why are you here?"

Can he be any more obvious? Roxy cut her eyes at me.

We've been sitting for two seconds, and he's already drilling him.

Maybe I shouldn't have invited Egan to eat with us. *I'd hoped he wouldn't be like this.* I had feared he would be, but I didn't know Brock all that well. We hung out together occasionally when my dad forced me, but he usually filled the time by talking about himself. I rarely had to add anything to the conversation.

"My kind have been hidden for so long." Egan grabbed his water and took a sip. "We thought it was time for us to assimilate back into the general supernatural population, and I wanted to attend college. I did some research and figured this would be a good place to get an education, and there are always a handful of supernaturals who attend here. It made sense."

Faint footsteps came from the woods.

I faced the trees. "I thought you said humans were afraid of this area."

"I did." Roxy leaned toward me. "But who's to say they're human?"

That's true. I hadn't considered it. At least two vampires attended here, though vampires didn't usually hang out in woods unless they were hunting.

The wind blew in our direction, and the familiar scent of rain hit my nose. Everyone grew silent, listening for who was heading our way.

Axel cleared his throat. "So, this girl ..."

Oh God. Were they talking about me? I forced myself to keep calm. I didn't need Brock or Roxy to figure it out if they were.

I couldn't see Donovan yet, but his tone held an edge as he said, "Don't know who you're talking about."

"Pink hair." Axel paused. "And hot."

They *were* talking about me. Luckily, I'd noticed a few girls around campus with colorful hair. I hoped that would keep me off their radar, but Roxy linked with me. *You little vixen.*

A low growl escaped Donovan.

It was odd. Humans didn't usually growl.

And he has it bad. Roxy stayed facing the woods, which saved Brock from being alerted that something was off. *Girl.*

"Did you just growl at me?" Axel asked with surprise.

"Uh ..." Donovan's head bobbed into view through the trees. "I did." He rubbed his hands together.

They walked the remaining several feet in silence.

They stepped out of the woods and startled, not expecting anyone to be out there. We should've made noise. Humans didn't stay quiet or still like we were.

Donovan's shoulders sagged when he saw who I was sitting with. He stepped toward us and winced. He opened his mouth to say something but stopped short when Brock stood.

CHAPTER SIX

"Can I help you?" Brock straightened his shoulders, staring at the two humans.

"Actually ..." Axel glowered at me.

"No." Donovan shook his head at his friend. "We were just finishing a hike, that's all."

"Are you sure?" Brock said mockingly. "You're staring awfully hard at Sadie."

"Oh, come on." Roxy waved her hand. "It's not her. Look at the amount of food piled in front of Egan. I've been gaping at it the entire time too." *You owe me big time.*

She'd demand a long explanation tonight. *I don't know what you're talking about.*

Maybe I need to stop helping these two humans out, Roxy goaded me. *I mean, let Brock chew them up and spit them out.*

"It takes a lot to stay in this kind of shape." Egan chewed a bit of food. "I work out hours and hours every day."

He was full of shit. That was one nice thing about being a shifter: strength, speed, and endurance came naturally. I had to tease him. "Well, it sure seems like you might be gaining some pudge on that belly."

"What?" He feigned shock. "Then, I'll add an extra hour next week."

"Maybe I should be there to spot you." Roxy flipped her hair around her finger. "You'll need someone to keep you accountable and honest."

"Are you serious?" Brock's face wrinkled with disgust. "Your family isn't—"

If I didn't stop him, he'd say something discriminating. "She broke up with you years ago. Stop pining for her."

"No—" Brock started.

"You need to accept that it's over." Roxy tried to hide her smile. "You can't still be hung up on me while attempting to date my best friend."

"Uh ..." Axel groaned and looked at Donovan. "Let's, uh, leave them to their dinner."

I couldn't blame him for being weirded out. This could pass for a scene in a soap opera.

"Sorry we bothered you." Donovan started toward the Student Center, but his eyes landed back on me. "You all have a good night."

His nice attitude caught me off guard. Was it because of the entire group or because of me? I felt like it had to be Brock and all of the animosity rolling off him.

I forced myself to take a bite like nothing was bothering me as the two humans headed off; however, I could feel Brock's gaze on me.

"What the hell was that about?" he growled when they were far enough away.

"You were about to run your mouth." I pointed my fork at him. "You can't go around talking about how Roxy can't make comments about Egan with humans in the area unless you wanna come off like a jealous ex-boyfriend."

"Why does it have to be ex?" Egan chuckled.

Roxy gestured to Brock. "Because there's no way in hell I'd ever date someone like him."

"Oh, please." Brock pretended to gag. "Like I'd be interested in a weakling like you."

"You fucking—" she began, but I cut her off.

This was going downhill and fast. "You two, stop it." They'd hated each other since they'd laid eyes on each other. "We all have to remember we're around humans." We'd all grown up around shifters. Even our high school was on shifter grounds.

"You're right." Roxy sighed. "Which I don't have a problem admitting, unlike some people here."

Egan continued eating, watching the meltdown going on. "I do have a question." He paused, drawing our attention to him.

"Sure." Brock took a sip of his soda. "We're all ears."

"Why does it matter if Roxy was hitting on me?" Egan asked slowly, choosing his words carefully.

"Because her father is the weakest shifter in Tyler's pack, and you're a strong dragon," Brock said condescendingly. "Surely you know that."

"Actually, I don't." Egan fidgeted in his seat. "So why is that? And what about humans?"

"Humans are definitely off the table." Brock scoffed. "They're so worthless and annoying. If not for their sheer numbers, we'd exterminate them permanently."

Instead of being straightforward, Brock still spoke in riddles. "What he's saying is that my family has proclaimed that only the strong can mate with the strong."

"Since when?" Egan seemed shocked by the information. "It used to be what most adhered to, but there isn't necessarily a law."

"It's relatively new." Roxy side-eyed Brock. "It was established in the last fifty years."

"Sadie's grandfather initiated the rule a couple of years before he passed away and Tyler took over." Brock beamed at me. "Her family saw how strong our race could become if we separated the strong from the weak."

Egan tore the crust off his pizza. "But isn't that kind of elitist?"

I could tell he wasn't happy about it, which made me curious.

"You'd be smart to listen and respect his decision." Brock didn't even notice that everyone but him was uncomfortable with this conversation. "Her family built most of the supernaturals' neighborhoods and businesses. If anyone knows how to hit the offender where it hurt, it's her family."

Roxy chewed her pasta in anger. *Wow, he's even more of a jackass than I realized.*

Oh, I'm not surprised. He'd been this arrogant as a child when I'd had to hang around him during annual alpha conferences among the packs. *I'm pretty sure he was born this way.*

She laughed loudly, causing Brock to go still. He asked her, "What's so funny?"

She stabbed a piece of chicken with her fork. "Nothing."

"Like hell it's nothing." Brock shifted his attention to me. "What is it, Sadie?"

"It truly was nothing." He didn't like people making fun of him. He'd beat up one of the betas at the last conference because of it. "She was laughing at the humans' reactions when they found us here."

An uncomfortable silence descended.

I needed to redirect the conversation. "It's not that supernatural races can't intermingle. They can even though we tend to stick to our own. And there are rare occasions when an alpha will mate with a weaker partner. However, humans aren't an option."

Egan chewed slowly and swallowed. "So, the entire supernatural race is divided into weak and strong?"

It wasn't quite that simple. Nothing ever was. "You could say it's a three-tier structure."

"That's fair." Brock bobbed his head. "You have the strongest, so think alphas and beta shifters, older vampires that have lost their humanity, priestesses, and strong wizards. Then, you have your middle tier where they aren't the strongest or weakest in the race, but they may have other redeeming attributes that would allow them to mate. And then you have the lowest tier. They're the omegas who can't hold their own, or their bloodline is so diluted that their powers have dried up."

"That sounds complex." Egan scratched his cheek. "I'm not sure where I'd fall in that structure."

Wow, a modest dragon. Who would've thought? "Dragons are right at the top."

"When Sadie and I inform her father about you, I'm sure he'll want to meet you." Brock pulled his phone from his pocket. "There was a rumor you had all died off completely."

"Obviously, we haven't." Egan ate some more, clearly uncomfortable.

He didn't sound impressed with everything he'd learned, which made me like him even more. "What do you like to do?"

"Believe it or not, I enjoy reading." He motioned to the trees. "And hiking. All the same things as you guys."

"And eating." Roxy motioned to his two trays, which were almost completely empty. "That was enough food to keep me stuffed for a day."

"Every shifter enjoys food." Brock chastised her. "Don't make it sound like it's unique to dragons."

I finished the last of my pasta and yawned. I'd enjoyed learning more about Egan, but Brock had made the whole situation uncomfortable. "I hate to do this, but I'm exhausted and have more work to do." *I don't think I can take being around Brock much longer.*

Girl, you and me both. Roxy stretched, following my lead. "Same."

"Go on and head back." Egan stood and grabbed my tray. "I can take yours and Roxy's trays back to the Student Center."

"Thanks." Roxy smiled as she climbed to her feet. "It was really nice meeting you."

"Same to you." Egan turned to Brock and frowned.

It was clear Brock had no intention of leaving. I felt bad for my dragon friend, but I had a feeling he could hold his own.

Roxy and I were watching television when my cell phone rang. I picked it up, and Dad's name flashed on the caller ID.

Great. Brock must have talked to him. I'd been kidding myself that he wouldn't tell Dad right away. "Hello?"

"Sadie," Dad said with annoyance. "I received an interesting call from Brock a few minutes ago."

"I'm good." I shouldn't run my mouth with him, but I couldn't stop myself. "Thanks for asking."

"Stop acting like a woman," he bit out. I could always count on good ole Dad for sexist comments like that. "Why didn't you call me earlier?" He didn't even sound the least bit remorseful. "You met a dragon, for God's sake."

"Well ..." I should've called him, especially if I'd planned on Brock meeting Egan, but he wouldn't have believed me until Brock had confirmed he was, in fact, a dragon. "I figured you'd want a full report from Brock first."

"Yes, but this is important. This will be a great opportunity for you to prove that you're worth something."

"How so?" I had no interest in proving my worth. I didn't want to go around threatening or killing people. That wasn't the type of person I wanted to be.

"You're a woman," Dad said slowly, "so you should be able to get him to spill his secrets like your mother did to me."

"But she died though." I didn't even remember my mother. She'd died during childbirth with me.

"That's not the point," he said angrily. "I need you to find out where they live, how many are alive—"

"Brock already tried." What did he expect me to do? "He doesn't want us to know."

"Then use your feminine wiles."

Wait. Roxy sat in her bed and faced me. *Did your dad just tell you to sleep with a guy to get information?*

"Are you serious?" I knew he didn't care about me, but he'd gone too far. "You want me to—"

"Stop being dramatic," he huffed. "This is our family legacy."

"How is this our family legacy?" I had to be missing something big if that was the case.

"We're going to rule over all the supernatural races soon, and to do that, some sacrifices need to be made." He seemed to be holding the phone closer to his mouth because his voice got louder. "And a dragon could cause issues if we don't learn what we need to from him. I need you to step up to the plate and get me that information. If not, there will be severe consequences." Dead air filled the line, effectively ending the conversation.

Roxy looked disgusted. "Your dad is the worst kind of scum."

"Yeah ..." That's all I had to say. He wanted me to seduce a dragon, and I hated to tell him it wouldn't happen.

THE NEXT MORNING, when my alarm went off, I almost hit snooze. I'd dreamed all night of Donovan, and I had no clue why. I couldn't remember the details, but the fact that I hoped to see him today didn't bode well for me.

"Oh my God." Roxy threw the covers over her head. "For the love of all things holy, turn the blasted thing off."

"It's nine in the morning." I got to my feet and padded over to my closet. "You act like it's the crack of dawn."

"It feels like it is." She rolled over and fell off the bed. "Dammit."

I spun around. "If that wasn't karma's way of telling you to get your ass up, I don't know what else it could be." I picked out a pink shirt and jeans. "Let's go eat breakfast together."

"Fine." She stood and rubbed her ass. "But only because I'm starving."

Within twenty minutes, we were entering the Student

Center. When we headed toward the cafeteria, a funny feeling took flight in my stomach.

"Are you okay?" Roxy glanced at me as we headed to the pancake line. *Something feels weird with you.*

I must have tapped into our pack bond without realizing it. *No, I'm fine.* Even if I wanted to tell her what I was feeling, I couldn't put it into words. *Just my nerves, for some reason.*

Probably because of your dad's phone call last night. She looked at me. *You aren't actually going to try to seduce Egan, are you?*

No, don't worry. I wasn't one of my dad's minions, and besides, I thought of Egan as a friend. *The dragon is all yours.*

That's not what I'm getting at. She got in line. *He treats you ...*

Donovan was several people ahead of us, and it was like he felt me approaching. He faced me, and our gazes locked. He pivoted forward again, not even acknowledging my existence.

This day couldn't get any better. *Look, I get it. And don't worry, nothing will happen.*

I sure hope not. Roxy didn't sound convinced.

Can we drop it? I really want to enjoy breakfast and get to class. I didn't want to worry about pack life. That was the whole reason we were here.

"You've got it." She winked and began rambling about clothes she wanted to buy on the internet.

I ENTERED Webster Hall in search of my biology class. I was going to be late, thanks to a certain self-proclaimed redheaded vixen forcing me to pick out her next outfit to order. Apparently, it was for the homecoming game in a few weeks.

Just like all the other classes, I was the last to arrive. For humans to be so damn slow, they sure knew how to get to class early.

There were ten tables in two rows in the entire room with a whiteboard right in front. The last open seat was in the front far left table. I headed straight to it and almost stopped when I realized who I'd be sitting next to.

Donovan.

Fate had to be mocking me. I forced my feet to move and trekked over to the chair.

He watched as I sat beside him.

I wasn't sure if I'd receive the nice, cold, or indifferent Donovan, and the worst part was, I wasn't sure which version I wanted.

CHAPTER SEVEN

My heart raced as I pulled a pink binder and a pen out of my backpack and placed it on the table. The chairs were so close that my leg accidentally brushed his when I sat back upright.

He jerked his leg away from me like I repulsed him.

This day was already starting out so lovely. I stared forward, wishing the professor would enter and begin class. The air between us held so much tension.

I tapped my pen on the table. I needed an outlet for all of this nervous energy.

"Do you mind?" he rasped but kept his attention forward.

"Uh ..." It took me a second to realize that the noise might be getting on his nerves. "Yeah. Sorry." One-word sentences were the best I had, apparently.

My leg bounced as the energy transferred to another extremity.

He glanced at the offending leg. "Too much caffeine this morning?"

"No." This was all due to his proximity, but I shouldn't

admit that. "I mean, yes." Side effects of caffeine sounded like a better excuse. "It was a long night."

His breathing increased. "Your group of four stayed out late?"

The fact he was interested enough to ask confirmed I wasn't the only one feeling whatever was between us. "No, Roxy kept me up last night, watching *The Bachelor*." I wanted to cry. I should've told him yes. The more we could discourage our connection, the safer both of us would be.

"Why am I not surprised?" A corner of his mouth lifted. "She seems like the type."

"Hey." No one insulted my best friend, at least, not in front of me. "She enjoys the angst. There's nothing wrong with that."

He lifted a hand in surrender. "Didn't say there was."

I had nothing to say to that. My wolf brushed against my mind, wanting to come closer to the front. Now wasn't the time. She probably wanted to go for a run or something; it hadn't even been a week but she was antsy. Back home, I'd go for daily runs just to gain some distance from my father.

"Are you okay?" he asked.

"Huh?" I wasn't sure what he was getting at.

"You seem uncomfortable." He turned toward me. "Are you feeling sick or something?"

"No ..." The fact he could sense my discomfort bothered me. "I'm just a little unsettled."

"What do you mean?" he started, but the door in the back of the classroom opened, and thankfully, the professor entered.

A week later, we were still playing the same song and dance. It was another Tuesday, and Donovan and I sat next to each other in biology class. We'd tried splitting up, but no one was willing to switch tables.

We'd been hostile and would avoid each other like the plague. This past weekend had been even more fun since he'd appear wherever we were.

"Beginning this week, Thursdays are lab days." The professor paced in front of the whiteboard and pushed his glasses up on the bridge of his nose. "Whoever you're sitting with will be your lab partner for the semester. Make sure to exchange emails or phone numbers. There will be assignments that you'll need to research together as well."

He grabbed a marker and wrote *the history of biology* on the board. A huge armpit stain caught my attention, which explained the horrid body odor I'd been smelling since the beginning of class. He wore a bright red shirt, so the area under his arms contrasted sharply.

"This is the first paper you two will write together. It's due by midterm." He pointed at the board. "Please research one topic that has been derived from biology and explain its impact on our world. I must approve the topic beforehand, so a week from today, you should have your ideas submitted to me. Class dismissed."

Not only would I have to be his lab partner, but we would also have to work on two papers together. Keeping my distance from him had already proven harder than I'd imagined.

I packed up my bag with no intention of giving him any of my information. The other students and the professor were already heading out the door.

"Here." Donovan handed me a piece of paper with his

number and email written on it. He tilted his head. "Where's yours?"

"I don't think we need to exchange info." If I had his information, I might be tempted to call him. This was the safest option for both of us. "We can talk here in class and figure it all out." I turned to stand and left his information on the table.

A huge hand grabbed my arm and kept me in place. "No."

My skin tingled where he touched me. I jerked my arm out of his grip, trying to keep my wits. "What do you mean no?"

"It's obvious you've had everything handed to you your entire life." His eyes darkened to a navy. "But I've had to work my ass off to get here."

"Wait." This asshole thought I was spoiled and entitled. "You don't even know me." I'd sacrificed a lot to get to this school. My dad had refused until I'd pointed out how all the alpha heir males went to college and I could possibly find a good mate here. I had no intentions of keeping that promise, but I'd been that damn desperate to gain space.

"It's obvious." He waved a hand at me. "You're gorgeous, dress well, and those two guys you hang out with have loads of money."

I must have misunderstood him. He couldn't have called me gorgeous. Even if he had, why was I hung up on this fact? "You think I'm gorgeous?"

"What?" His cheeks turned pink. "I ... uh ... you must already know that. But don't worry, you're not my type."

That stung and woke me from my stupor. "Thank God."

I picked the paper up from the table, and he sighed with relief. I smirked and leaned forward, ignoring his sweet, rainy smell, ripped the paper in ten different sections, and dropped it to the ground.

He blew out a breath, and the scent of his minty toothpaste filled my nose. The combination of his distinct smells almost undid me.

"It figures." He stood, slung his beaten, black backpack on his shoulder, and turned his back to me in dismissal.

I shouldn't ask, but there was no stopping me. "What does that mean?"

"You don't give a shit about anyone but yourself." He faced me again, disdain etched into his features. "Apparently, it doesn't matter to you that I grew up in the system with no one in my corner. I scraped and fought my way here, but sure, piss it all away for me."

No wonder he was so hardened, but that didn't give him the right to insult me and act like it was okay. "You don't know shit about me." I stepped into him and shoved my finger into his chest. "My life isn't as peachy as you'd like to think. Brock is the price I had to pay to get here." I needed to stop, but he enraged me like no one ever had. "And last week, my dad told me to sleep with a guy to get information, so don't act like you're better than me."

He stumbled back a step. "Are you serious? Your dad wants you to ..." He trailed off, disgusted and unable to finish that sentence.

Why in the hell had I told him that? I'd never, ever hinted that my dad was an asshole to anyone other than Roxy. The one time I broke down was with a human I was incredibly attracted to. "Just ..." I grabbed my bag and sucked in sharply. "Forget I said anything." I didn't want to face him again. I'd already said too much.

I hurried to the door, barely able to keep to a human speed.

"Sadie ..." he called after me, but there was no way I'd stop.

I'd been so stupid to tell him all of that, but my mouth had run on its own accord. That had never been a problem before. Hell, I'd never put anything that bluntly to Roxy, so why him?

His footsteps pounded behind me, but he couldn't catch up. I pushed through people, being rude as fuck, but I didn't care. It was bad enough knowing I'd see him tomorrow, let alone right now.

Outside, I rushed to the tree line. I needed to be one with nature and get back some semblance of my life.

"Sadie," Donovan said, closer than he should've been.

I spun around to see that he was only twenty feet away. That shouldn't have been possible. No human could be that fast ... could they?

Nothing about him made sense. I shouldn't have been that attracted to a human—they didn't affect me in ways I couldn't control—and I shouldn't have had a loose tongue with him.

The closer I got to the woods, the more I tapped into my animal. I gained distance from him. At this point, there was no telling what I might say to him. It was safer for me to run away. I hit the trees and let my wolf push forward, but not enough to shift. I had to get deeper into the woods before I let the animal side of me take control. He didn't need to find my bag and clothes. That would only lead to more problems.

My nerves calmed as the trees flew by. With each step, the fresh hair filled my nose, eliminating *his* smell. Around five miles deep, I tossed my backpack to the ground and stripped my clothes. I called my wolf forward, and my bones cracked as light pink fur sprouted across my body.

When I stood on four legs, I took off, running deeper into the woods.

***

SADIE? Roxy linked to me.

I'd been running for God knew how long, but this was exactly what I'd needed. I trotted next to a long stream I'd found deep inside the woods. This was probably farther than most humans went during the week. *Yeah?*

Where are you? She sounded very concerned. *We're here at the Student Center, looking for you. I thought you'd be grabbing us a table.*

I'm sorry. I'd forgotten all about our lunch plans. They all had a noon class, and we were supposed to meet up at one-thirty. *I forgot all about it. I'm actually in the woods. Give me ten minutes, and I'll meet you there.*

Are you okay?

Yeah. I'd tell her about everything later, but not around our vampire friends. I hadn't known them for long enough. Trust had to be earned.

I pushed my legs, running fast toward the university. Donovan should have given up looking for me by now.

The last few miles, I let my tongue hang out, enjoying the breeze. It wasn't long before I was back where I'd left my clothes. I shifted back to human and got dressed. Right before I stepped out of the tree line, his scent hit my nose like a freight train.

"Sadie," Donovan said, not even ten feet away from me. He rushed toward me, scanning me from head to toe.

"What are you doing here?" He should have been back at the dorm or somewhere that wasn't here.

"Looking for you." He reached his hand out.

I flinched.

"Hey," he said softly. "I won't hurt you." He slowly touched my hair and pulled his hand back. There was a twig in his fingers. "I thought you wouldn't want to wear this in your hair all day."

"Uh ..." I'd never felt so awkward in my entire life. "Thanks?" I hadn't meant for it to sound like a question.

"Why in the world did you run out here alone?" He surveyed the area. "You need to have at least one other person with you out here at all times."

I started to laugh but realized he wasn't kidding. "Oh ... I grew up in the woods."

"Really?" His brows pulled together. "I didn't see that one coming."

"Because I had everything handed to me on a silver platter?"

He nibbled on his bottom lip. "Maybe I spoke out of turn, but that doesn't matter." His jaw clenched. "You still can't run out here alone. It's reckless. You could've gotten hurt."

"Then, you could have found a new lab partner." Humor was best in these types of situations. "That would have been a solid win for you."

"I don't want one like that." He huffed. "I definitely don't want you injured."

I wasn't sure how to respond. "Well, I've got to go meet Roxy, Katherine, and Lillith."

He dropped the twig to the ground. "Is that your group of four females?"

"Yeah." I motioned to myself. "As long as you're including me in that number."

Neither one of us spoke, and we stared at each other.

Sadie, Roxy said in a panic. *Are you okay?*

Shit, there was no telling how long we'd been standing here like this. *Yes, be there in a second.* "Look, I've got to go. Thanks for your concern." I spun on my heel and headed back toward the Student Center, leaving him in the woods.

Inside the cafeteria, I found the three of them already together at a booth. I hurried over and grimaced as I slipped into the seat beside Katherine. "I'm sorry, guys. I needed to go for a run and lost track of time."

"In the middle of the day?" Roxy's forehead wrinkled. *With humans out and about.* She had two Philly steak sandwiches in front of her, and she plopped one on an empty plate and pushed it my way.

Thank God. I was starving. "Yeah, last class was intense." There wasn't another word I could use for that.

"How so?" Lillith took a swig of her blood, which was again in a coffee cup with a lid.

"No reason." My voice went high-pitched, and the air began to smell.

"Dude." Roxy wrinkled her nose. "I'm trying to enjoy my meal here. Stop making it smell all up in here."

A few guys next to us chuckled. One of them said, "Is it sad that she's still hot even if she has no problem passing gas in public?"

Katherine burst out laughing.

And I'd thought my awkward years were behind me.

The front door opened to the Student Center, and Donovan walked in. My eyes were glued to him. Maybe coming here had been one huge mistake.

CHAPTER EIGHT

R oxy followed my gaze and snapped her fingers in front of my face. "Earth to Sadie."

Somehow, I tore my attention from Donovan and focused back on her. "What?"

"You seem to be focusing on"—Lillith tapped her index finger against her bottom lip—"someone your dad wouldn't approve of."

No truer words had been spoken. "I heard the door open and was curious who'd entered." That wasn't a complete lie, but I had been drawn against my will.

"Sure, let's go with that." Katherine slurped her drink.

"Ew." Now that had my full attention. "Please, don't. I can't stomach it."

Lillith rolled her eyes. "Like what you do is much better."

Roxy motioned to the vampires' cups. "We don't do that."

Lillith leaned across the table and lowered her voice. "You eat raw meat sometimes."

"Nope, this isn't happening here." With our luck,

another supernatural would enter the seating area and hear us discussing this topic in a room full of humans. "You can never be too careful."

The scent of brimstone swirled around us right before a hulking presence appeared beside us. "Very smart girl."

Lillith's eyes widened, and she hissed. "Are you what I think you are?"

"You know what?" Staying here was a bad idea. We needed to move away from everyone. "Why don't we go sit outside the library again?" *Apparently, those two can't keep their mouths shut today.*

"Sounds good to me." Roxy took the lead and stood. "Same place as last time. Wanna join us after you get your food?"

"Would love to," Egan said with an edge. "We have something we need to discuss."

"Is everything okay?" I wondered if the conversation with Brock a week ago had cast us in a negative light. Now that I thought about it, he had been missing. For him to leave, it must have affected him more than I'd anticipated. "Did our dinner last week upset you? You kind of disappeared."

"Oh, no. Not at all. He was the ass, not you two. I just had to go back home. It's something else. I'll be out there soon." He glared at the vampires before heading to the cafeteria.

"What the hell is his problem?" Lillith scooted across the bench seat. "I've never even seen the guy before."

"You should be focusing on the most important part." Katherine brushed past me. "They knew about that guy and didn't tell us."

"Damn ... you're right." Lillith bobbed her head. "You got some 'splainin' to do."

"Just wait." Those two had trouble figuring out when they should shut up. I turned on my heel and led the group out the door and toward the library.

Two large groups of people sat outside. In one group, guys were kicking around a hacky sack while the girls sat and watched. The other group sat at a table, deep in conversation about a party this weekend. What I wouldn't give to have that kind of life. I'd hoped to achieve a carefree life by coming here, but it was obvious it wouldn't happen.

The seats behind the library were again vacant.

"I wonder why no one is out here." Katherine stopped for a second. "There aren't any sounds of humans anywhere, except inside the building."

"That's because several wild animals were seen roaming the woods." Roxy took a spot next to the woods. "Someone was going on this morning about how a guy went into the woods with a girl last night and never came out."

"Are you serious?" The woods were a haven for the supernaturals here, so there shouldn't have been anything threatening nearby. "I didn't smell anything strange or feel any threats."

"You know how humans can be." Lillith lifted her cup, wielding it like a weapon. "They make up shit just to start drama and spread rumors."

"Supernaturals are just as guilty." Now that I'd gained some distance from Donovan, my stomach growled with hunger.

"True." Katherine glanced over each shoulder and sat across from Roxy. "Before he gets here, is he a fucking dragon?"

"Sure is." Roxy motioned for Lillith and me to come sit. "Apparently, Sadie and he have a class together."

I took the spot next to Roxy. "He seems nice. He ate dinner with Brock and us last week."

"The snobby wolf guy?" Lillith wrinkled her nose. "Someone needs to put that guy in his place."

"According to my dad, he's excellent mate material." Somehow, I'd said that without gagging. I impressed myself. "Never in a million years. I'd rather run away and marry a rat shifter."

"Don't blame you there." Roxy shuddered. "He might be the antichrist."

I almost choked on my food and reached for the extra bottle of water on Roxy's tray. I took a few swallows, washing down the hard lump. "The antichrist is supposed to be charming."

"Then that eliminates that possibility." Roxy took her last bite. "I mean ... he's awful."

Movement caught my eye, and Egan stepped out from behind the building.

Like last time, he carried two trays completely full of food.

"Damn." Lillith's mouth dropped open. "Did you buy the entire cafeteria out?"

"Those jokes never get old," he deadpanned as he headed over to us. His shoulders were tense, plastering his light blue shirt against his muscles even more. Something had to be bothering him, but I had no clue what.

Make room for him. I hated to make the vampires sit next to him. Fear shone in their eyes even though they were trying to play it cool. Dragons weren't known to have even-tempers.

He might eat you, Roxy warned but made room for me, leaving half the bench open for him.

I patted the spot next to me. "Here, join us."

He set his trays down and did just that. His pupils turned into slits when they settled on the vampires. "I'm surprised you two can go out during the day."

Wow, he'd wasted no time confronting them.

Lillith inhaled sharply. "What do you mean by that?"

"Just saying that some of your friends here can't." He grabbed a hot dog and bit it in half.

My heart dropped. Were there more vampires here without the noblest of intentions?

"We're the only two here from our nest." Katherine chewed on her top lip. "Are others of our kind here?"

The fact that they weren't lying comforted me greatly. It seemed to do the same for Egan since his body relaxed.

"Let's just say I was out for a run last night and stumbled upon a girl with her fangs in a guy's neck close to campus." His arm brushed mine as he lifted his drink. "He'd be dead if I hadn't interrupted her feeding. She heard me and ran, so I didn't see her clearly."

"Shit." That would cause issues if students were going missing. "They aren't supposed to eat where they live if intermingling with humans."

"I've never been part of this civilization, and my thunder knows that golden rule." He lowered his voice. "I get that the supernatural world doesn't value humans as mates, but that doesn't mean they should be treated with disregard."

"Our nest agrees with that." Lillith pointed at the sun glaring down on us. "Obviously, or we wouldn't be sitting here with you right now."

Egan tilted his head. "The fact you're telling the truth is your only saving grace."

"Any idea who it could be?" I didn't know many vampires, so my resources were limited.

"No." Katherine tugged at her lip. "But we could do some digging."

"Is the guy okay?" Roxy's face was lined with concern. "Did he get turned or worse?"

"Luckily, she didn't feed him her blood, or I would've had to do something." Egan scratched his head. "If there's a new vampire here, it isn't safe for anyone."

A newly turned vampire had no problem drinking human or supernatural blood. Only later did their taste buds become fine-tuned enough to only crave humans.

"I carried him to his dorm." He closed his eyes and sighed. "He'd lost so much blood. He was confused and couldn't remember anything. I'm assuming she messed with his brain before she chowed down, but we need to find her before this becomes a regular occurrence."

"We rob the blood bank periodically ..." Katherine started.

"Shut up," Lillith hissed. "We don't need everyone knowing."

"Do you actually think that's a well-kept secret?" Roxy chuckled. "Every supernatural knows that little trick of yours."

"Fine." Lillith breathed. "We might have extra for a vampire who's in a pinch."

"She seemed to like drinking from the tap." Egan looked at me. "Even the moonlight bothered her."

"Then why is she here?" Normally, if they'd gone that dark, they could live just fine without an education.

"No clue." Egan tapped his finger on a tray. "Either way, it can't be a good thing."

THE NEXT MORNING, Roxy, Lillith, Egan, and I met outside of the Student Center thirty minutes before our classes began. Katherine had an earlier class, so she couldn't be part of our meeting.

"Did you find anything out?" Egan asked.

"No, we'll have to do some digging." Lillith adjusted her tight-fitting black dress. "It's not like my group knows everything about the others."

"I can see if my dad knows anything too, but I'll have to be strategic." If my dad got a whiff of a vampire that dark was here, he'd be down here in a heartbeat, trying to recruit her for the awful side jobs he needed people with no conscience to perform. "It won't be a fast answer."

"That's fine. We need to be careful, but in the meantime, I'll keep a patrol. No one else needs to get hurt." Egan glanced at his wrist. "I'm going to grab something to eat. Will the three of you go check out the tree line to make sure nothing happened last night after I fell asleep?"

"Yeah, see ya," I said as I waved, and the three of us headed toward the woods.

"Why is he so big on protecting humans?" Lillith whispered.

I wanted to smack her since there were people around, but the damage had already been done. "I don't know." It was odd. Most supernaturals cared more about not being discovered than protecting humans.

"Maybe his kind doesn't discriminate like ours." Roxy shrugged. "Who knows?"

"That would be so strange, though." Before humans and other supernaturals began tracking them down, dragons had been the most powerful race. You'd think they'd want to end up back on top, but worrying about humans wouldn't put them there.

We walked half a mile into the woods from the border, and after another quarter of a mile, something metallic hit my nose.

"Do you smell that?" Please, God, let me be imagining things.

Roxy frowned. "Yeah."

We picked up our pace, and between two large bushes, we found a small puddle of blood. It could easily have been from a vampire or animal eating something. The blood had congealed, so the trail of whoever had done this was cold.

"Should we tell Egan?" He already acted overly concerned, so I'd hate to tell him when it could be nothing.

"No, not yet." Lillith squatted and sniffed the area. "I think this was an animal."

"Okay, but maybe we should come back here after classes. We can meet at the cafeteria." I hated to disregard it and have it turn out to be something. "We can go over the area again to see if we missed something." We had ten minutes before classes started.

"Sounds good." Roxy motioned for us to follow her. "Let's go."

THE NEXT TWO classes passed without much of an issue. Egan asked if we'd found anything, and I told him the truth and that we would look into it more later. He would meet up with us to help scour the area to make sure we hadn't missed anything.

My heart hammered as I climbed the stairs to my psychology class. It, unfortunately, had everything to do with Donovan. A human held too much control over my emotions.

Like last time, I entered the classroom, and the seat right in front of him was the only one open. I wished something had changed, because the more time I spent with him, the more I was drawn to him. I hadn't confided that little fact to anyone.

I took my seat and pulled out my classroom items. I refused to start a conversation with him. Luckily, the guy who'd hit on me the first day now avoided me. My wolf took joy in that.

"Hey." Donovan's breath hit the back of my neck. "You haven't taken any more random walks alone, have you?"

The concern in his voice thrilled me. "No, I haven't." I turned so I could see him.

His blue eyes were bright, making my breath catch, and his gaze landed on my lips. "Good, I couldn't have something bad happening to my lab partner."

I licked my lips before I could stop myself. "You might enjoy a bigger group." This had to be the most civil conversation we'd ever had. "Less work that way."

"Nope, I have a hard time getting along with people." He leaned back in his seat, putting some much-needed distance between us. "So, it would be an extra person I'd have to tolerate. You're the lesser of two evils."

"Wow." I giggled. "You're such a sweet talker."

"I've been that once or twice." His face scrunched up like he smelled something disgusting. "This is the face that really does it for them."

"I can see why." This felt so normal and comfortable. How had we been at odds before? "It's the less awkward looking of all the expressions I've seen so far."

"Well, thanks." He grinned. "I aim to please."

I could think of some serious ways he could please me.

My body warmed at all of the thoughts. Ugh, down girl. That couldn't and wouldn't happen.

He grabbed a pen and doodled on the clean sheet of paper. "So, we do need to discuss our paper topic."

Now I felt like an even bigger asshole for tearing up his phone number and email address. "Yeah, you're right." Everything inside me told me not to do it, but I wrote my phone number down and handed it to him.

He started and took the paper gingerly like it might bite him. "I was thinking maybe we could meet up and brainstorm together."

I opened my mouth to tell him no. "What about the Student Center tonight?" What the hell? That wasn't even close to no. He'd been an ass to me. I had to remember that.

"What about ..."

He didn't have to say anything more. I knew exactly who he was talking about. "Brock has a night class." It'd been a pleasant surprise that I hadn't been around him as much as I'd feared when coming here. I thought he'd be monitoring my every waking moment, but between our class schedules and football, I had time to breathe.

"Okay." He rubbed his chin. "Six?"

"Sounds great." This was my first meeting with a guy like this, and of course, it was with a human who made me feel things I shouldn't.

CHAPTER NINE

I should have been running to meet up with the others to scour the woods, but here I was, hanging back after class had been dismissed, hoping to talk more with Donovan.

I wasn't being smart, but I couldn't get myself to leave.

He slung his backpack over his shoulder and grinned. "Is this your last class of the day?"

I hadn't noticed before, but he was dressed in black slacks and a white button-down shirt instead of his usual jeans and t-shirt look. "Yeah, it is. Are you going somewhere?" I wanted to take back the words, but I couldn't. I was ready for him to retort that it was none of my business.

"Yeah ..." He diverted his attention to the ground and huffed. "I've got a job interview I'm heading to now."

"Oh ..." I'd forgotten he'd mentioned looking for a job. "I'm guessing Axel is happy about that."

His eyes flicked to mine. "Why would you say that?"

Shit, I had to stop hanging around him. I kept saying stupid things. I shouldn't have been able to hear their conversation. "You said that you had to scrape by to get here. I ..." I was at a loss for words.

"That makes sense." He followed me to the door. "I'm being paranoid. Yeah, he will be. He's got a few interviews lined up too."

"Are you guys roommates?" I didn't understand why I couldn't stop asking questions. I was probably coming off like a stalker.

"Yeah. Are you and your redheaded friend?" he asked as we walked into the hallway. His arm brushed mine, and goosebumps spread across where he'd touched.

I slowed my pace to match his. "Her name is Roxy, and we are." Maybe he wanted to prolong our time together.

A comfortable silence descended between us as we walked past the double doors.

As I stepped outside, my spine tingled, alerting me that I was being watched. I looked toward the woods and found Lillith, Roxy, Katherine, and Egan there, waiting on me.

He chuckled. "I take it your friends are here for you."

"Appears so." I took a step in their direction and stopped, glancing over my shoulder. "Good luck with the interview."

"Thanks," he replied with warmth. "I'll see you soon."

"Okay." I forced myself to turn back and head toward my friends.

Roxy's forehead lined with concern. *What's going on?*

Great, she was suspicious. *Nothing.* Thankfully, I wasn't close enough for her to smell my lie. That would change in the next few seconds, though. *We were talking about our biology paper and how we needed to pick a subject.*

Maybe you should change partners.

I reached them. *Too late. The professor assigned partners, and we were put together.* I left out the part where I had to sit with him, which was asinine. It was the only seat available.

"Okay." Egan gestured to the library. "We should enter down there instead of in front of all the humans. We don't need anyone suspicious to follow us."

"Can't we eat first?" Roxy asked in defeat.

"How many times are you going to ask that?" Lillith shook her head.

"What happened to meeting at the cafeteria?" I had hoped to eat before doing this as well.

Katherine pursed her lips. "Egan got too impatient and said we needed to search first. You were taking too long, so we came to find you."

"The longer we wait, the colder the trail gets," Egan explained as he marched toward the library. "Let's hunt, and then we can get something to eat."

Walking beside me, Roxy touched my arm. *What is up with this weird obsession?*

No clue. He was upset over all of this. *But after Brock's twenty questions, I won't ask. I figure he'll tell us when the time comes.*

Maybe. She increased her speed since we were falling behind. *He's kind of secretive.*

Can you blame him? It had been decades since anyone had even spotted a dragon. They had to hide to stay alive.

Nah, I guess not.

We reached the entrance to the woods at the back of the library, Egan still taking the lead.

Right before he was ready to enter the tree line, he stopped. "Where did you find the blood?" He realized he had no clue where to go.

Lillith took lead and entered the woods. Taking a left, she headed toward the site of the blood. "Over here."

As she increased her pace, we kept up with her. It wasn't long before we found the small break of trees where the two large bushes were located. She moved some branches back, revealing the blood.

I faced him. "I'm thinking it's animal."

"Yeah." Egan relaxed. "You're right."

Katherine chewed on her thumbnail. "It sounded like you scared her off the other night."

"Maybe." He walked behind the bushes and examined the area. "But she could've thought I was human."

"She wouldn't have run if she'd thought that." Lillith tapped her nose. "She must have caught your scent, so she should hold off for a little while."

"But she could go somewhere else to hunt," he spat. "So humans aren't any more protected."

"You seem awfully concerned." Katherine dropped her hands. "It makes sense that you're worried about the humans here. The more occurrences happen here at the university, the harder it is for us to go unnoticed, but you've taken it a step beyond that."

Roxy elbowed me in the side. *I'm so glad it wasn't one of us who asked the question.*

Don't be too glad. Egan didn't seem thrilled with the vampires even though he was being nice to them. This question could make things more tense.

"Look, I get that your culture doesn't care about the weak." Egan stilled and tapped his fingers on his khaki pants. "But I know what it's like to have your breed attacked and almost die off."

I hadn't considered that, and it put things into perspective. Even though my dad wouldn't be overjoyed with his point of view, I got it, and dammit, I respected it.

"That makes sense." Lillith patted his arm. "The

problem is that you can't save every human. Yes, she might go elsewhere to feed, but we don't know where. Maybe if we keep an eye on the papers, we can figure it out."

"Good plan." Egan gestured toward the cafeteria. "I guess there's no point in staying out here any longer. Let's go grab something to eat, and we can take it from there."

Without needing any additional encouragement, our group sprinted back to campus.

"Okay, what gives?" Roxy dropped her history book on her bed, keeping her place, and glared at me.

"What are you talking about?" I sat at the desk, tapping my pencil on my paper. I'd been staring at my calculus homework for over ten minutes and couldn't concentrate worth a damn.

"You've been tapping that pencil for God knows how long." She leaned back on her pillow and crossed her arms. "So, what's on your mind?"

I'd been dreading this conversation, but it was inevitable. "It's nothing, but ..."

She lifted an eyebrow. "But?"

"As you know, I have that paper with that human." If I used his name, it would make it sound more intimate. "And we need to work on it."

A coy grin crept onto her face. "Independently, via emails?"

The bitch. "He wants to meet in person."

"When?" She closed her history book, making it clear that her focus was solely on me.

"Oh ... I don't know." I flipped the pages of my notes.

The more I convinced her it was nothing, the more she'd drop it. "Maybe tonight. I can't be sure."

"That's problematic." Her jaw set. "How will you determine whether it's tonight or not?"

"Maybe we should go to the Student Center earlier than the normal time. How about we go around five or something?" I kept my gaze on my notes.

"Why not our normal time?" She leaned on an arm. "No point in going early if you aren't even sure you're meeting him. Unless ..."

"Fine." It wasn't like I could get out of this without telling her. "I'm meeting him at six."

"Why would that matter if it's only for a school project?"

"You know how he is." Brock would make a scene.

"Are you sure that's the only reason?" Her face tightened with concern. "You've always acted differently around him, and the way you were acting earlier, you never looked more happy."

If I lied to her, she'd know. "I don't know what's going on." My frustration rang in my words. "I feel a connection to him."

"You were at each other's throats, and you aren't anymore. What happened?"

"He thought I was a spoiled princess, and I told him I wasn't." I regretted opening up to him that way. Us hating each other had been easier.

"And he just took your word for it?" Roxy stood and closed the distance between us. "That's hard to believe."

"I might have told him about my conversation with my father ... the one we had our second night here." I winced, prepared for the fallout.

"You did what?" Her mouth dropped, and she stood over me. "That's not how humans act with their kids."

"He won't know." I hadn't realized how bad it was until now. "He grew up in foster care."

"Look, I get it; he's hot." She scooted closer to me. "But he's human."

"It's not a date." It took me saying it for me to realize I wouldn't mind it being one. I had lost my mind. "It's honestly a school project."

"Well, I'll be nearby." She paced in the walkway between our beds. "You can't do something stupid. You know your father—"

"I know." I didn't need her telling me that he wouldn't hesitate to kill me. He'd enjoy it. "Nothing is going to happen. This is a one-time thing."

She stopped and stared right into my eyes. "You sure?"

"Yeah." It had to be. For the next paper, we'd have to work out the details in class or something.

"Okay." She snapped her fingers. "I'll be there with you. I don't need him stealing your virtue."

"My virtue?" We'd gone from talking about biology papers to him spreading me out on a table and devouring me in front of all the students eating at the cafeteria. "I'm pretty sure it's already gone." It wasn't like I was a virgin.

The fact that me having sex with him actually sounded enticing should have bothered me, but my brain was going down a pretty raunchy road.

"Oh my God." She waved her hand in front of her nose. "What the hell are you thinking?"

My cheeks felt like they were on fire. "Nothing." She would never let me live this down.

"Like hell it's nothing." Her eyes bulged, and she

pointed at me. "You were thinking of him claiming your virtue."

"Just stop." I couldn't even meet her eyes. "We're meeting in the cafeteria. There will be no virtue taking."

"Damn straight because I'll be watching you like a hawk." She pounded herself on the chest. "And I won't allow it to happen."

"It wouldn't happen even if you weren't there, but okay." I laughed because, otherwise, I'd be crying. "You can stay as long as this conversation ends now."

"Fine." Her face softened. "Your dad has given you hell all your life. I just want to protect you if I can."

And that was why she was my best friend. She might be snarky, high maintenance, and annoying at times, but she had my best interests at heart. "I know. I love you."

"I love you too." She hugged me and leaned back. "Now, just because you can't date him doesn't mean we can't drive him wild."

And the next two hours went by at a snail's pace as she treated me like a real-life Barbie.

"Okay, it's time." Roxy put the brush down and motioned to the mirror.

My makeup wasn't drastically different from normal, but she'd brought out my features better than I could. She'd curled my bob, making my hair more bouncy, and forced me to wear a cute, light blue wrap dress. It brought out my eyes and complemented my hair.

"Why did you get all dressed up again?" If she could give me shit, I would dish it back. She'd worked on her hair and makeup just as much as, if not longer than mine. Her red hair cascaded in waves down her back, and gray eyeshadow made her eyes pop. She'd slid into a black catsuit that looked amazing on her.

"Just need to look my best at all times." She flipped her hair over her shoulder and sashayed to the door in her black stilettos. "And hey, if I could catch Egan's or another supernatural's eye, maybe I could get lucky tonight."

"Nope, remember: we aren't losing our virtues tonight," I said parroting her words back at her.

"Girl, you know that ship has sailed." She winked at me and opened the door. "Come on, let's go get something to eat. I'm famished."

We entered the Student Center. A few guys catcalled Roxy, but she ignored them. I scanned the room and found Donovan sitting at a booth in a back corner, his eyes locked on me.

Over here. I headed straight to him, paying no attention to anyone else around me. When I reached the table, Axel lay against the wall and cleared his throat.

Apparently, Roxy wasn't the only one concerned about our meeting.

"Sadie," Axel acknowledged formally and sat upright alert.

Donovan glared at him. "I hope you don't mind that my dumbass friend insisted on coming."

"No, it's fine." I gestured to Roxy beside me. "She demanded to come as well."

"We are eating, right?" Roxy placed a hand on her hip. "Because I'm starving."

"Why don't you two grab us some food so Sadie and I can talk biology for at least a few minutes?" Donovan said as he stood so Axel could get out. "Just get me a burger and fries."

"Fine." Axel slid across the seat. "We'll be back in a minute."

Behave. Roxy warned.

You're getting food and coming right back. I considered killing her in her sleep tonight. *I can't get into too much trouble.*

Damn right. I'll be back. She shoved past Axel and swung her hips as she left him behind.

Maybe I wasn't the one she should be concerned about. It sure looked like she wanted Axel's attention.

A large, warm hand brushed my arm, and I turned to find myself almost flush against Donovan.

He glanced at my lips, and a musky animal smell mixed with rain filled the air. Wait ... that wasn't from me but him.

He smelled like a wolf.

I took a deep breath, needing to make sure, but it disappeared without a trace. I had to be imagining things, but inside, my wolf whimpered.

CHAPTER TEN

"Hey, are you okay?" He almost touched my shoulder but stopped short. Whatever he saw cross my features must have unnerved him.

"Yep." I forced the words out and tried to downplay my obvious hallucination.

"Are you sure?" he pushed, not buying my ruse.

"It's stress." It had to be. I wanted him so bad that I'd just projected wolf-like attributes onto him. "This is all so new and a little overwhelming."

He put his hands into his pockets. "With a dad like yours, I'm sure it would be."

"What does that mean?" I might have slipped and told him a few things, but how had he read into it so much? I hadn't meant to make him pity me.

"Nothing." He laughed without humor and rubbed a hand over his face. "Growing up, bouncing from foster home to foster home, you learn how to read people."

"Really?" I couldn't believe he was trying to bullshit me. "So, I went from silver-spoon princess to being controlled and weak?"

"Not weak." He pinched the bridge of his nose. "But I hadn't considered silver-spoon princesses could go hand in hand with having a fractured relationship with your father."

He rattled me to my core. The fact that he was human and reading me like this wasn't good. He observed things he shouldn't, which meant this was a big mistake. "Look, how about our paper be about fossil fuels? We can talk about the waste it gives off and global warming."

"Yeah ... okay." He opened his mouth then stopped. He pulled at his ear. "I didn't mean to—"

Roxy appeared beside me with a tray of food. She looked from him to me. "Is everything okay?"

"We were just finishing up." I needed distance and fast. I turned my head and found Katherine and Lillith entering the Student Center. "And there are our friends. They must be looking for us." I grabbed Roxy's arm and hauled her away.

"Hey, Sadie!" Donovan called after me.

My feet stopped of their own accord. Stupid traitors. I glanced over my shoulder.

He tugged at his ear again. "Are we okay?"

The concern wafted off him. This whole situation sucked. If I'd been human or he'd been a wolf, we could have acted on the attraction between us. "Totally." I turned back around, desperate to stay but also get away. It felt like two halves of me were at war.

Totally? Roxy mocked as we made our way to the vampires. *When did you begin talking like that?*

I purposefully said the next words, trying to get her to focus on something other than what had gone down. *Bite me.*

Good try, but even though I love ragging you about your love of vampire puns, it won't work. She waved the vampires over as we took a table in the corner away from Donovan and Axel. *What the hell happened after I left?*

She wouldn't stop until she got the truth. *I could've sworn his scent was musky for a second, and then he proceeded to talk about my father and how it must be hard being away on my own after growing up like that.*

Damn ... She snorted, and her shoulders shook. *The two of you are a hot mess.*

Exactly. It hurt to admit, but the truth smacked me in the face. *Which means I need to stay as far away from him as possible.*

That's what I told you earlier. She stood tall. *It feels so good to say I told you so. It doesn't happen to me very often.*

For someone so adamantly against him, you sure made a point to dress up even more than usual. That could only mean one thing. *You thought Axel would be there.*

Her face fell. *What? No!*

The stench of rotten eggs filled the air. *You bitch. And you gave me such a hard time.*

"Hey, guys," Roxy said a little too enthusiastically. "What brings you here?"

"Food ... of course." She lifted the cup in her hand. "We stopped to get a drink before coming here."

In other words, they had to keep up the illusion of being human.

"Sounds good to me." Lillith walked over to the round table for four. "This is perfect, anyway."

"Everything okay?" Katherine sat between Lillith and me. "You seem upset."

"It's nothing." I didn't want to talk about it anymore. "So, have you heard anything?" Steering our conversation toward corrupt vampires should make them focus elsewhere.

"Not yet." Lillith frowned. "Our only hope is stumbling upon her here."

I picked up my chicken sandwich and took a bite. "We could walk around and look for her. She could be hanging around here after her night class or something." If a morally compromised vampire like that attended here, she wouldn't have a choice but to take night classes.

"That's not a bad idea." Katherine sipped the blood. "She'd either be around here or at the library."

"Or gym," Roxy added.

"Which is connected to the library." We'd been stalking the perimeter there, anyway. "It wouldn't hurt."

It was after six but late August. It didn't get completely dark until around nine, so we had time to kill before then.

My favorite scent in the world filled my nose.

"Hey, Sadie." Donovan sounded unsure. "Can I talk to you for a second?"

Say no, Roxy commanded. *Just say no.*

I turned to face him, forming the word "no," but I stopped.

He rubbed his neck and bounced his foot. "Please."

The *please* did me in. "Okay."

Roxy glared at me. *That was not "no."*

He's my lab partner. At least I had that excuse working in my favor. *I can't be a complete jackass.*

"You have five minutes." Roxy leaned back and scowled at him. "That's it."

"Come on." The longer we stayed with her, the more she'd embarrass me. I stood and felt a tingle down my spine. I turned to find Axel glowering at me.

Both our best friends were in full protection mode.

"Let's go outside," Donovan said with annoyance. "Otherwise, they'll watch us the entire time."

I followed him outside and away from the people congregating outside the main door.

He faced me and took a step closer than necessary. "Did I offend you? I didn't mean to step over the line."

"No, you didn't." I was softening toward him, which would be problematic. "You see too much."

His forehead creased, and he nibbled on his bottom lip. "How so?"

I wanted to be honest with him, so I had to be careful how I played this. "You're right. My relationship with my dad is complicated, to say the least, but he's not the type of man to go against."

"To go against?" He laughed. "Who said I wanted to go against him?"

"No, I know you didn't, but my father doesn't like me hanging out with just anyone." I was walking a thin line. "They have to meet his strict criteria, and if they don't, he won't allow it. That's why Brock is here."

"To tattle to him?" Donovan lifted a brow. "Why would he be willing to do that? Is he family or something?"

"No, but his family wants to align with mine." I almost gagged. I hated everything about my world. "So, Brock was more than willing to come watch me."

"That's not normal." He took another step toward me, leaving only a small space between us. "I'm guessing I'm not the caliber of man he wants for you, and that's why you're putting distance between us."

"Putting distance between us?" I could barely hold in my giggle. "We only recently stopped fighting. But, no, that's not why. I don't want you to get hurt."

His blue eyes darkened. "Are you promised to Brock or something?"

"What? No." I'd never agree to mate with someone like

Brock. "Never. I'd rather be on the run my entire life than settle with a douchebag like him."

"I just thought your dad was pressuring you or something. But as long as he isn't, I'm okay to take the risk." He licked his bottom lip. "If you are."

"I can't date you." It was time to put the limitation out there. "It would be like a death sentence for you."

"Well, then it's a damn good thing I don't find you attractive." He smiled sexily. "Then I might be screwed."

The scent of a lie spread through the air, which made me way too happy. "I'm serious." Yet, I couldn't move away from him.

"Me too." He lowered his head, and his minty breath hit my face. "We have to work together on this stupid paper."

The alluring scent of arousal made me dizzy. "It's a damn shame."

"It would be better if we were at least friendly," he whispered. His breathing became rapid as the tension between us thickened.

I wanted to kiss him so badly. The only thing holding me back was his safety. If it weren't for that, I would've closed the distance between us and worked out my sexual frustration. Maybe if we got it out of our system, we could move on.

The door behind us opened, and Axel's rainy, peppery scent hit me. I stepped back before he spotted us.

The corner of Donovan's eyes crinkled with confusion. "Is everything—"

"Hey, man," Axel said, and Donovan looked in his direction. "Your food's getting cold."

"Yeah, man." Donovan's gaze landed back on me. "I'll be there in a second. We're wrapping it up."

"Okay." Axel watched us for a second longer before heading back inside.

Donovan scanned my face, searching for something. "How did you know he was coming outside?"

This was why I didn't need to be around him. He was too damn observant. "Years of walking on eggshells." I'd meant it as a joke, but it fell flat.

He grimaced. "Damn, that was bad."

"I realized it after it came out." Things felt too natural between us. "But I couldn't take it back."

Sadie, I'm about to march out there, Roxy warned. *I've gracefully given you six minutes instead of the threatened five.*

It was a good thing she had my back. Right now, she prevented me from making a worse mistake by staying out here.

"Look, we better go back before Axel and Roxy come and drag us in by our ears." I tried to keep my tone light. "But we have our research topic." I spun on my heel and stepped toward the Student Center.

"Hey, wait." He gently tugged my arm, pulling me beside him. "I got that job earlier today."

"Congrats." I'd been so self-centered. "I should've asked. I'm sorry."

"No, that's not what I'm getting at." He chuckled and didn't remove his hand from my arm.

The longer we were together, the more I felt a connection to him. "Then, what are you getting at?"

"Wow, I'd always thought I'd be smoother than this." He let me go and chuckled as he glanced at the ground. "Maybe you can come by after my shift one night to work on the paper?"

"Wait, you're inviting me to come watch you work?" And, hot damn, it enticed me.

"In all fairness, it's after my shift. Since I'm training, I get off earlier, and they encourage us to hang around and watch the more experienced waiters. Besides, I invited you to the Student Center to work on our paper, hoping to sneak in a meal." He shrugged and held out his arm. "You see how well that went. I'm thinking getting you to come to Haynes Steakhouse is a more solid plan."

"Solid?" That was the worst idea I'd ever heard. "Really?"

"Yeah, maybe not so much, but I can give you the employee discount on your meal." He closed his eyes and shook his head. "Oh my God. Just forget it."

"No." Steak sounded delicious, and the meals here were mediocre. "I'll come. When are you thinking?" I had to be strategic.

"My first night is Friday, so let's do Saturday." His face brightened before dimming again. "If you don't have plans, that is. You probably want to go to the Black and Gold game."

"Nope, I definitely do not." And that meant Brock would be preoccupied with the game. "That works out perfectly."

"Okay, great." He grinned.

"Sadie." Brock's pretentious voice grated my ears. "What are you doing out there?"

I fought against the urge of tensing and acting guilty. "Discussing a class project." I turned to face him, lifting my chin. "Did you get out of your class early or something?"

"Nope, we're just on a break." Brock scanned the area. "Where's your *best friend*?"

"She's inside, eating dinner." It hurt not to be a complete ass. "I'm about to go join her."

"That's a very smart idea." He took my arm and pulled me to the door.

I wanted to fight him, but he might try to hang around me more if I did. I turned back for a second and waved at Donovan, refusing to act like a jerk.

Donovan frowned but nodded. He didn't seem thrilled about the recent development, but he didn't push. Thank God.

Inside the Student Center, Brock didn't let go of my arm. Instead, he dragged me past Roxy and the vampires and down the walkway. We entered the deserted hallway in front of the closed bookstore.

He spun around with a look of disgust. "What the hell was that back there?"

My wolf howled inside me. "No, the right question is: What the hell are you doing manhandling me in front of everyone?" I might be submissive to my father, but I wouldn't submit to him.

He scoffed. "I'm an alpha heir."

"As am I." Yes, they didn't take my claim seriously since I was a woman, but whether they liked it or not, I was all my dad had. "And if you ever touch me that way again, I won't be so complaisant."

"Do you know what your father would say if he saw what I did?" he asked with disdain.

"Seeing as we're going to a mostly human school, I expect he'd be smart enough to realize I'd be paired with one on some projects." He was being an idiot. "Obviously, I can't say the same for you."

We glared at each other until he looked at his watch.

"Fine, you're right." He blew out a breath. "I was out of line."

I almost stumbled back from shock. I hadn't expected him to admit it.

"But that guy was looking at you with more interest than a school project, like he thinks he has a shot with you even though he's a weak-ass human," he grumbled. "It pissed me off. I was angry at him, not you."

"Well, he doesn't understand how things work." I had to tread carefully so he didn't catch me in a lie. "We both know he and I could never be together."

"You're right." He took a few steps back toward the door. "I've got to get back to class. We can catch up tomorrow."

I stayed back and watched him disappear toward the Student Center's doors. My heart pounded way too loudly over what he'd said. Donovan wanted me. For some reason, Brock catching on to it made it more solid ... more real. The problem was that I wasn't sure I could stay away from him any longer.

CHAPTER ELEVEN

"Tonight is perfect for watching for the vampire," Egan said as he paced in front of the library as we girls sat at the table.

"It's the huge Black and Gold scrimmage game." Roxy ran a hand over her body. "Which means I get to dress all cute and enjoy the sight of bent-over football players."

Tonight was an important milestone that kicked the school year off at Kortright. Our football team would split into two teams and play one another.

"I'm thinking we aren't going." Lillith pouted. "He's going to have us staking everything out and working."

Egan stopped and scowled at those two. "This is more important than some pointy shoes and belly revealers."

"Pointy shoes and belly revealers?" Katherine burst into giggles.

"What?" Egan frowned and scratched the back of his neck.

I bit the inside of my cheek, trying not to embarrass the poor guy more.

"What the hell are those?" Roxy's face twisted like she was staring at an alien. "Do I even want to know?"

"The shoes that look like you could fall over and break an ankle in." He pointed at the heel of his tennis shoe and moved it to his belly. "And the shirts show your belly skin."

"Where did you come from?" Lillith scoffed. "They're called high heels or stilettos, depending on heel size, and the belly revealers are either crop tops or belly shirts."

"It bothers me that you think I actually care." Egan cringed and flexed his fingers. "This is life or death and more important than whatever those are called."

Roxy sucked in a breath.

"He's right." They would derail his whole point if I didn't help him out. "There will be other football games you can dress cute for once the vampire is caught or no longer a threat."

"Of course you'd agree with him." Roxy glared at me. "You don't want to go because of Brock."

"Can you blame me?" The less he could watch me, the more freedom I had. "He made a big enough scene the other night when he found me talking to Donovan outside." Saying his name made my heart skip a beat. Ugh, I shouldn't be going to see him tonight, but he'd looked so cute yesterday when he'd asked if I was still in. I was supposed to be there at six, right around dinner time. He was working the lunch crowd until he got enough experience to move to the weekend dinner rush.

"Don't think you're getting out of helping." Roxy threw a hand up. "If I don't get to enjoy the game, then your sorry ass can't be holed up inside the dorm."

"All hands on deck," Lillith agreed. "You can scour the tree line or something."

"Uh ..." I had hoped to get out of helping because of the

game. I hadn't even considered them wanting me to stand guard. "I can't." I winced. Here we go.

"And why the hell not?" Roxy crossed her arms. "It's not like you have plans ..." Her lips parted. "You do and didn't expect to tell me."

"Wait ..." Egan looked at me. "You aren't planning to help?"

Now I had to do damage control. "No, I plan to. I just need to meet up with someone first. I'll be back right after the game starts." It had conveniently worked out this way, but I wouldn't let it slip that I hadn't purposely planned it that way.

Roxy cocked her head and lifted an eyebrow. "Who are you meeting?"

"Like you don't know." Lillith snickered. "If I was a betting woman, I'd lay down a hundred dollars on that pathetic human who keeps sniffing around her."

"That's the problem, though." Roxy stood and pulled at her navy shirt. "He doesn't sniff. If he did, we wouldn't be having this conversation."

"Excuse you." She had a point, but I wouldn't address that. "We tried working here on campus, and you and Axel descended on us like flies on poop, and then Brock showed up, making a scene. We're going to work on the project over steak."

"Flies on poop?" Lillith snorted. "That's a fairly accurate description."

"Shut it, bloodsucker," Roxy spat.

Poor Egan stood there, blinking.

"You two, calm down." Katherine sighed. "She's going to eat and come back here to help. I doubt she'll get pregnant in public."

"You didn't see all the eye-fucking going on," Roxy grumbled.

I knew what would defuse the whole situation. "I'll bring you back a steak."

Roxy placed her hands on her hips. "You have my attention."

The best way to get on the good side of a shifter was through their stomach. "Fine, I'll bring back two for you and three for Egan." I kind of felt bad for leaving him hanging too.

"Fine." Roxy ran her fingers through her hair. "I guess I can make a one-time exception since it is in public, you have a project, and there is steak involved."

"But you'll be back in time to help us keep an eye out after it gets dark?" Egan stared at me with so much hope. "It'd be nice to have your help."

"Yes, I'll be back by eight-thirty." I'd make sure of it. Donovan should be fine on his own.

"Okay, we can scout out things around the stadium, and when Sadie gets back, she can stake out the perimeter of the woods." Egan nodded. "Hopefully, nothing will happen, but we need to be prepared."

"Great, now we can go relax before we work all night." Roxy yawned.

I Ubered to Haynes Steakhouse. The building was older but had brand-new charcoal blue siding. It had two dark, cherry wood doors with a bronze sign perched above it. Mercedes-Benzes, BMWs, Lexus, and other high-end cars were sitting in the parking lot.

For a second, I considered leaving. I wore dressy-casual

clothes—black slacks and a white belted shirt—which was the bare minimum dress standard for a place like this. But I didn't want to hurt or upset Donovan like that. Even though he was rough around the edges, there was something about him I didn't want to ruin.

"Ma'am." The driver sounded annoyed. "We're here."

"Oh, yeah." I pulled my phone from my purse and added a tip. "Thanks."

As soon as the door shut, the driver sped away.

My phone showed it was five after six, which meant I was already a few minutes late. Roxy had given me the rundown on ways to ensure this didn't turn into a date. She was being ridiculous. He'd asked me here to accomplish two things: knock out schoolwork and watch what to expect on his job.

I approached the doors, and a guy my age opened it for me and waved me inside. "Welcome to Haynes Steakhouse," he greeted.

"Thanks." The restaurant reminded me so much of the places Dad conducted business. He didn't favor chain restaurants or the super upscale but the ones in between. They garnered the least amount of attention.

The hostess smiled. "Hi, how many will be joining your party tonight?"

"June, she's with me." Donovan's raspy voice washed over me.

"What?" The hostess pouted as she glanced from him to me. "I thought you were single."

Subtle was not her name.

"Yeah, I am." He didn't take his eyes off me. "But hopefully, not for much longer."

My body warmed, and I took a step back. Roxy was right. This wasn't smart.

"She doesn't seem interested," the hostess quipped.

"That's where you're wrong." He strolled over to me, his blue eyes deepening to navy as he scanned me.

Between his words, the snug black slacks that left little to the imagination, and the white button-down that hugged his body, danger surrounded me. I wanted him so damn much.

"I got us a seat in the back." He took my hand and laced his fingers with mine.

I should've pulled away, but I didn't. I didn't know where we were sitting, so I needed him to guide me.

Yes, denial fit me comfortably at the moment.

The restaurant had booths along the walls and several tables scattered throughout. The restaurant was packed, but the seats were spaced out enough that it didn't feel over-crowded. The tables were covered in sturdy, white table-cloths, and chairs were made of thick dark maple.

A server who had to be another college student took an order. When he finished, he turned, and his green eyes landed back on me.

He put his pen in his white pocket and jerked his head to the side. His brown, shaggy hair curved to the side.

Even though I was around humans, I instinctually took the side of the booth against the wall. I didn't need someone sneaking up on me. "It looks like a lot of people who work here attend college. Do any go to Kortright?

"No." Donovan slipped into the other side of the booth across from me. His back was to the rest of the restaurant. "They go to the local community college around here."

"Oh, shit." It went against everything inside me, but he was supposed to be watching his coworkers. "You probably should sit here."

"Nah, it's okay." He moved his silverware to the side

and smiled. "I'm good here. How's your day been?"

"Good." I couldn't hide my smile. "Aren't we here for schoolwork?"

"Yep." He nodded at me right when a guy appeared.

"Well, well, well." The guy smirked at Donovan. "What do we have here? You get off work and decide to hang around?"

"He's staying to watch you all like he was asked." That had to be obvious, but then it hit me.

"Is that what he told you?" The guy tsked. "Donovan, I thought you had more game than that."

"Shut it, Chad." Donovan didn't sound impressed. "I'll take a Coke."

"Okay." He nodded and gazed at me. "And you, gorgeous?"

Donovan's nostrils flared, and he glared at Chad.

"A Coke sounds good for me too." My stomach rumbled. "Do you know what you want?"

"Yeah ..." Donovan rattled off his order.

And it was my turn. "Okay, I want the largest steak you got, medium-rare, and when we're close to finishing here, I'll need five more of them to go."

The waiter froze. "Are you serious?"

That request sounded crazy now that I thought about it. "Yup. My friends back at campus are chomping at the bit for this."

"Okay, I'll go put this in." He walked off.

"Wow, you love meat, don't you?" Donovan placed his arms on the table.

There wasn't a good way to answer that. I needed to say something, but I had no clue what.

"God." He grimaced. "I wasn't being a pervert. Did I come off like that?"

It took a second for it to click. "No, but now that you mentioned it ..."

His face turned pink. "I honestly meant ... like cow meat, not my meat." He smacked his head on the table, and the plates rattled.

I laughed harder than I ever had in my entire life. Tears pooled at the corners of my eyes.

"So you're enjoying yourself?" An embarrassed smile crossed his face. "I have to admit it's nice to see, but I wish it wasn't to my detriment."

"I'm sorry." It was nice to be around someone as socially awkward as me. "But ... confession time. Why are we here? Obviously, it isn't for you to watch your coworkers."

"Honestly, it was at first. My boss recommended it the other night." He nibbled on his lip. "But seeing you at the hostess stand, I decided I wanted to be off duty."

"For this to be a date, you have to ask me." I needed to be clear that we weren't on one. "I came here for schoolwork."

"But you didn't bring your stuff either." He motioned to the purse I'd brought.

Dammit, I hadn't even considered that I needed the backpack. I'd been too wrapped up in seeing him that it hadn't crossed my mind. "We talked about this."

"We did," he agreed. "But every time we're together, I forget why we shouldn't try to make this work between us."

God, those words sounded so damn good. "Then maybe ..."

"I know you feel it too. You wouldn't have come without your backpack otherwise." He reached across the table, and I placed my hand in his. "I've never let anyone in, and it's scary. But maybe ... it'll be worth it."

"My dad ..." I let his name hang in the air. "He won't—"

"You're strong and gorgeous," he said and leaned across the table, captivating me. "Why don't we take it slow and see if there's anything to consider fighting for?"

I should have removed my hand from his, but I couldn't ignore whatever brimmed between us. "Fine. But just friends." That's all I could give him, and even that was a risk.

"I'll agree to that ..." His eyes twinkled. "... for now."

"All right, here you two go." Chad set our appetizers and drinks down in front of us. "I'll go put your to-go orders in now."

I HAD TOO much fun at dinner. We laughed, and Donovan told me stories about his and Axel's shenanigans growing up. The night felt perfect in every way.

Of course, that was when fate decided to be a bitch.

A sickening sweet smell filled the air and pulled my attention away from him. My eyes landed on a girl with almost translucent skin, dark hair that hit the small of her back, and eyes that were dark and soulless. My bones chilled.

I linked with Roxy. *There's a vamp here.*

She stood in the hallway, surveying the area like she was on the prowl. She was looking for trouble, and I was the only other supernatural here.

Do you think it's the one we're after? Roxy paused. *Wait ... you're still at the restaurant with him?*

Waiting on your steaks. It was a good thing she wasn't around to catch my lie. Yes, I was waiting on the steaks, but that wasn't why I'd stayed so long. *Ask Egan if her skin was so translucent it glowed?*

Chad hurried past her toward us with the steaks I'd ordered to go. He set them down on the table. "Here you go. You two are set."

"Uh ..." I focused on the waiter. "I haven't paid yet."

"He took care of it," Chad said and gestured at Donovan. "Dude, you gotta get better at this."

"You paid for the steaks to go?" The fact he was short on cash and had still done this both upset and flattered me.

"Okay, this is awkward, so I'm going to go." Chad saluted me. "It was nice meeting you."

"It's no big deal." Donovan shrugged. "Besides, I was a dick to you, especially about your eating habits. Consider this my big apology."

"Not again." I couldn't be mad at him, but I didn't want to take advantage of him. "But thank you."

"You're welcome," he said tenderly.

He said yes. Roxy connected back with me. *That's what stuck out in his mind as odd.*

Then it's her. I should have been relieved I'd found her, but not here and not now. Not with Donovan. *I'm at Haynes Steakhouse.*

We're already in Egan's car and heading that way.

"Hey, you," the vampire cooed at Chad. "I'm having car problems, and I was hoping I could use a phone in here or something. There wasn't anyone at the front, and you're the first person I've come across."

The rotten stench wafted off her, hitting me hard several tables away. She was lying.

"Sure, let me go look at your car." Chad grinned. "I'm on break now anyway."

"It's behind the restaurant." She motioned toward the back exit.

"Oh, okay." He huffed. "They won't let us go out back, though. We'll have to walk around from the front."

"That works," she purred and strolled to the front of the restaurant with Chad following dutifully behind.

I jumped to my feet, refusing to let Chad out of my sight. "Let's go."

"Are you okay?" Donovan grabbed the bag and stood behind me. "You seem upset."

"Nope." I glanced at my watch. Shit, time had flown with him. It was eight-thirty, and I was supposed to be at the game, which meant it was getting dark outside. "I'm just late meeting up with my friends." I didn't waste time hurrying to catch up with the two of them.

"It's odd that June isn't up here." Donovan scanned the hostess desk. "She's not supposed to disappear without someone covering for her."

The doorman turned our way. "Yeah, I went to the bathroom and when I came back she was gone."

My stomach revolted. Maybe I'd caught her scent too late. Could she have feasted on the girl? The thought made me walk even faster.

When we got outside, Chad was about to turn the corner with the vampire.

"Chad!" I yelled, desperate to catch his attention before it was too late. I cursed Roxy as I ran toward them in these dumbass high heel shoes. Donovan followed right behind me.

Chad paused and turned around. His forehead creased as he watched me approach. "Do you need something?" Surprise rang in his voice.

"No, I just ..." Shit, what did I want? I couldn't really say, "To save your life."

The vampire spun around, and she scowled.

A red ring around her pupils indicated she'd recently fed. It had to be June. "Your boss was asking for you back there."

"What?" He glanced at his watch and looked at Donovan. "Really?"

I hadn't even considered Donovan might rat me out.

"Yup. Said you didn't tell him about your break," I interjected, hoping to God that Donovan would follow my lead.

"Shit, she needed help with her car." Chad's shoulders sagged. "I forgot. Do you two mind helping her?"

"No, man." Donovan sounded a little off, but he was going along with my lie. "We've got this."

"Thanks." He winked at the girl. "Sorry about this, but you're in good hands." He hurried back into the restaurant.

The vampire scowled at me.

If I'd had any doubts before, they were long gone. She had fed on June and tried with Chad.

"Where's your car?" I tried to sound innocent, but we both knew what was going on.

"You know what?" She pulled her phone from her pocket and swiped. "My brother just messaged me. He'll be here in a second."

"Are you sure?" Donovan stiffened, and he planted himself right next to me as if he felt the threat. "We can—"

"No, it's fine." She spun on her heel, rushing to get away.

"Oh, and be careful." She had to know we were on to her. "We wouldn't want you getting into any trouble."

"Don't worry." She glanced over her shoulder, her face full of hate. "I can take care of myself."

That was the problem. If she took care of herself, everything I had here would be at risk. Now, I had to figure out how to explain this whole thing to Donovan.

CHAPTER TWELVE

"Hey, are you ready to go?" Donovan lifted the bag of to-go food. "I'm assuming your friends will want this before it gets cold."

"No, not yet." I needed to make sure that bitch at least got in the car and drove off. She'd fed off one person tonight, so I hoped this would scare her off for the rest of the night.

A vampire truly only needed to feed once a day, and even then, they didn't have to kill. They could drink several pints and be satisfied, but vampires were gluttons. A chill ran down my spine. June had to be around here somewhere, drained, and we needed to find her body before a human did.

It made me sick that she'd drunk so much and had been going in for a second kill. If I hadn't been here, Chad would probably be lying next to June right now.

The vampire glanced over her shoulder and snarled when she saw me watching her.

Did the stupid bitch really think I'd rush away?

She got in her Mercedes-Benz sedan and started her

car. The engine purred, proving her car issues had been a ruse.

Roxy linked with me. *Hey, we're almost there.*

She's on the side road, behind the restaurant. I hated not staying here to help out, but I didn't need Donovan asking more questions. *I'm getting Donovan out of here.*

That's a good plan, Roxy agreed. *The vampire is still there?*

Yeah, she's expecting me to leave. My stomach dropped. *I'm pretty sure she killed the hostess, so there's a dead body hidden somewhere.*

A Jeep pulled up behind the vampire.

Okay, we're behind her. Roxy waved at me from the passenger seat. *Go on and head back.*

"Do you mind giving me a ride?"

He looked past my shoulder at the Jeep. "Is that your friend?" He shouldn't have been able to see Roxy from here with his human eyes.

Maybe a joke would disengage him. "Roxy must be so hungry she's projecting her image in your mind."

"Ha, she probably can." He stepped toward the parking lot, turning his back to the vampire. "And of course, I don't mind giving you a ride back. We're going to the same exact place."

"Okay, that would be perfect, then." I caught up and walked beside him. "I had to Uber here. Dad didn't want me to bring my car to school." He thought it would make me less likely to go anywhere without Brock. He didn't know much about Uber since he had drivers.

"It would be my honor." He grimaced. "But you can't judge me for my car."

"Is it that bad?" I tried to focus on the moment between

us. *Is everything okay?* I didn't want to leave if Roxy was headed into a horrible confrontation.

Yeah, she pulled off. Roxy laughed. *When her eyes landed on Egan, she must have recognized him because she took off before we could even get out of the vehicle. We're going to look for the hostess now.*

Let me know if you need me. I could always run back here.

Donovan led me to an older, light gray Toyota and opened the passenger door. "Here you go, ma'am. Your humble chariot."

Even though it had years on it, it was well kept and still smelled new. My eyes landed on the deodorizer hanging from the rearview mirror. I settled onto the tan cloth seat and took the to-go food from him.

He shut the door, hurried around, and slipped into the driver's seat.

"Hey, I think they gave us too much food." I'd ordered five steaks, but there were six containers inside.

"Yeah, when you went to the bathroom, I had him add in something for Axel and paid." He winked at me as he started the car. "I didn't want to get hell for not bringing him something back, especially if he found out about the five steaks you got Roxy." His voice went up at the end, almost like a question.

"Well, two of them are for Roxy." I hated to tell him that he'd bought food for another dude.

His body stilled. "I didn't buy that asshole food, did I?"

"Brock?" I asked.

"Dear God." He groaned, and his head sagged.

"No, you didn't." I touched his arm. "Just Egan, but he's a good guy."

"I'm not sure if that makes it any better." He focused on

where my hand touched his arm. "Is he someone I should be worried about?"

"We're just friends, so why would you worry?" I dropped my hand, forcing myself to listen to my own words.

"Yeah ... right." He took my hand in his. "Friends who don't see other people."

I should correct him, but I couldn't force myself to. The thought of him with another girl made me irrationally angry, and my wolf growl.

A cocky grin spread across his face as he shifted the car into drive and pulled out of the parking lot. "Want to tell me what all that was back there?"

"What do you mean?" I wasn't sure what to say if he pushed the whole Roxy question.

"Between you and that odd girl." He turned onto the main road that led back to campus. "It looked like you two knew each other."

I had to tread carefully. No, I didn't know her, but we'd recognized each other as supernaturals. But I couldn't say that. "Not really. We know of each other, but we don't hang in the same circles. She's kind of a troublemaker."

"She looks like the kind." He rubbed his nose. "And she smelled overripe and was pretty but in such an odd way. Almost ghost-like."

He could smell that? Granted, the worse off they were, the sweeter their scent, and she had reeked. It was like they were overcompensating for their rancid souls. And he'd pegged her skin color correctly. "Yeah, she's been causing trouble."

"Well, I don't know Chad, but he seems all right." He placed his arm on the center console, our skin brushing. "It was really nice of you to watch out for him."

"I did it for more selfish reasons." I didn't want humans

to find out about us. "I'd hate for him to get hurt when I could at least try to protect him."

The large brick buildings of Kortright came faintly into view.

We found the missing girl. Roxy linked with me again, disgust evident in her voice. *There's no blood left in her.*

Even though I'd expected it, my stomach still soured. *Was it only her, or are there others?*

Only her. Granted, if you hadn't followed her, I'm sure she'd have kept going. Roxy growled. *She didn't just drain her. The girl's neck is broken too. It's like she played with the body or something.*

That made it so much worse.

"Are you okay?" Donovan looked at me. "You got a little pale."

"No, I'm fine." I had to stop talking to them. *When do you think you'll be back?*

We put the girl in the restaurant's dumpster, and we're going to light it on fire so the police can't tell the girl was bitten. Roxy sounded worried. *Egan is pouring gas on the body right now.*

Are you sure that's a good idea? That could end in disaster.

Too late, Roxy said. *It's done. We're back in the car and on our way to get you. We need to see if we can track this bloodsucker down.*

I had a feeling this would make the news. If they hadn't burned the body, her death would've done the same thing but for different reasons. *Okay, meet me in the Student Center.* Luckily, most of the students would be at the game.

Donovan pulled into the dorm's parking lot and turned off his car. "So, I guess this is it."

"Thank you for dinner." This officially felt like a date.

"I can walk you to your room." He motioned to the girls' dorm. "Or are you going to the Black and Gold game?"

"Neither." I'd given up on having a normal college experience. We were supernaturals, for God's sake. "Roxy wants to go out and explore the town. I'm not super thrilled about going to the game since Brock's on the football team."

"Well, then, I'm glad you aren't going."

"Are you heading to the game?" From what I'd learned, humans enjoyed football games, and I was sure he could find himself a girl to spend the night with.

"Nope, I don't like crowds." He tucked a piece of my hair behind my ear. "And I'd only be interested in going if you were there."

My breath caught as he leaned over the center console. His eyes focused on my lips. I forced myself to breathe, which wasn't smart. His rainy scent made my head fuzzy.

Pulling away would have been the right thing to do, but I was at his mercy. I licked my bottom lip, and he sucked in air.

He leaned over a little more, leaving only an inch of space between us, and paused for a second before moving slowly once more.

My brain yelled at me to move, but I couldn't hear it over the loud thumping of both our hearts. When his soft, warm lips touched mine, my tongue ran across them.

A loud groan left him as he opened his mouth, allowing my tongue to enter. His minty taste mixed with steak exploded in my mouth, and I moaned as our kiss deepened.

I'd been kissed before by other shifters, but never with a non-shifter. And all previous kisses paled in comparison to this moment. My wolf howled, surging forward, and my hand wrapped around his neck, tugging him closer to me.

Our lips parted, and our tongues stroked each other. All

sanity had left my body, and his touch and how he felt under my fingers were what mattered to me.

Hey, we're about to pull in. Roxy linked, pulling me back to reality.

I sighed and pulled back, and I almost lost it again when his hooded eyes met mine and the spicy scent of his arousal filled my nose. "I'm sorry." It hurt, but I forced the next words out. "We can't."

"I agreed with you until now." He smashed his lips together and cupped my cheek. "I feel something for you. Something I can't control. And I know you feel it too."

"But ..."

He placed his finger on my lips. "I'll be patient, but I won't give up. I've never wanted to fight for something so much in my entire life."

His words thrilled me, and my wolf whimpered with happiness. The fact that my wolf wanted this too baffled me most of all. It didn't make any sense.

"Roxy will be here in a second." I didn't know how else to respond. I didn't want to encourage him, but I didn't want to discourage him either.

He leaned over me, almost making my heart jump out of my throat.

"What are you ..." I whispered.

He pulled out the top container from the bag. "Getting Axel's food." He laughed and opened his door. "But it's good to know you liked the move."

Oh, dear God. He knew I liked it. I opened my door and jumped to my feet. "No, I thought you were hurt. I was scared."

"You thought I was hurt?" He arched an eyebrow and looked at me smugly.

Something about his attitude made him even sexier. It wasn't fair.

"Yes." The air around us reeked from all the lies falling from my lips. With how keen his senses were, I needed to tone it down. He might think I was farting up a storm and not want to get near me again. "Maybe a heart attack or something."

"If anyone was going to have a heart attack, I'm pretty sure it'd be you." He closed the distance between us. "All I ever see you eat is meat."

"We're back to discussing meat again?" I had to shut him down and fast.

"Touché." He grinned as he reached into the car and pulled out my bag of food, handing it to me.

A Jeep pulled up beside us, and the passenger-side window rolled down, revealing Roxy. Disapproval lined her face. "What's going on here?"

"Nothing." I lifted the bag of food. "By the way, Donovan got these for you two."

"Really?" Egan leaned forward and nodded. "Thanks, man."

"Uh ..." Donovan frowned at the dragon. "Yeah."

Egan stared at me intently. "Look, we need to get going."

"Yeah, okay." I faced Donovan and suddenly felt regret. I had to go with them to find the vampire, but I didn't want to leave. I'd never been torn like that before. "I'll see you later."

"Sure." Donovan nodded, but his attention stayed on Egan. "Are you sure you don't want to hang out with me?"

"Nope, she's coming with me." Roxy got out of the car and opened the back passenger door, revealing the two vamps in the back.

"You're making me get in the middle?" Lillith frowned but scooched over, not waiting for an answer.

I looked one last time at Donovan, and anger seemed to be pouring off him. I wasn't sure what was going on, but more important things were at stake. "I'll see you later?"

"Yeah, okay." He slammed the door shut and stalked off toward the dorms.

"Well, that was pleasant," Roxy said as she climbed back into the car. "Come on, Sadie. We've got to go."

I wanted to go after him, but that wasn't possible. We had to track down a vampire.

CHAPTER THIRTEEN

Egan pulled away, but I kept my eyes on Donovan as he marched toward the dorm. He was pissed, but I couldn't leave my friends hanging. I got that this situation wasn't ideal, but we'd had a good night together. My lips still tingled from our kisses.

"You keep turning your neck like that, it'll break," Lillith joked, then turned serious. "You do realize you and him can't happen, right?"

"Yeah, I know." I really did, but my heart refused to accept it. I understood that I needed to put space between us, but I didn't know how. We had two classes together and were lab partners. My wolf didn't even want to be away from him, which made the struggle even harder.

"Girl, if you keep this up, you'll dig your own grave." Roxy turned in her seat and pointed her finger in my face. "I'm not trying to be a bitch, but if you care for him, you need to stay away."

I wanted her to piss off, but she was only looking out for me. I had to remember that. "You're right. I don't know what's going on, guys, but ..." I didn't want to tell them about the tug. It would make Roxy angrier.

"He's hot as hell, just like his buddy." Roxy flipped back around. The air conditioning blew her hair back in my face.

I smacked it out of the way. "So, I'm not the only one drooling over a human." She'd stepped into that one all on her own.

"But I'm not putting myself around him," Roxy retorted. "So don't even try to compare us."

"No, you two just stare at each other with hate and lust," Lillith said and elbowed Katherine in the side. "Am I right?"

"You're getting too much pleasure from their situation." Katherine leaned forward so she could glance at me over Lillith's body. "Just ignore her. She loves stirring up drama."

"Once you've lived for over two hundred years, then you can lecture me on what you find entertaining." Lillith lifted her head with her nose held high.

"So what if you're attracted to a human?" Egan turned back onto the main road, heading toward Haynes. "I don't think it's a huge deal."

"Her dad would never allow her to even kiss a human." Roxy snorted loudly. "If she did and he ever found out, the guy would be dead in seconds."

"Why?" Egan's hands tightened on the steering wheel. "I still don't get it. Yes, they're not strong like us, but they have a heartbeat just the same."

I hadn't ever considered that, by him and me merely kissing, I could be putting his life in jeopardy. My dad had eyes and ears everywhere. I was being reckless, and my life wasn't the one at stake.

"Because your mate represents your strength just as much as you do," I said, repeating the words Dad had told me over and over again. "If you align yourself with a weakling, you're no better than them and must be treated as such."

"Whoa, never heard you talk like that before." Lillith lifted a brow. "Here I thought you might be more grounded than your father."

"No, that's what he tells her almost weekly." Roxy rubbed her arms. "I've heard it as often as she has. He was pissed when she and I became best friends."

"Really?" Egan looked at Roxy. "Why?"

"Because my father is one of the lowest pack members." Roxy kept her eyes on the road. "Therefore, I'm considered weak. Sadie is expected to surround herself with only the strongest."

"People like Brock." I hated the elite sector of the supernatural society so much. They were arrogant know-it-alls who thought of women as mere possessions. My father was determined to pick my mate and for him to be the alpha heir instead of me. He didn't want a woman leading his pack. "The kind who refuse to admit they're flawed and imperfect."

Lillith tapped her lips. "It'd be handy if you could just bite him and turn him."

"She could." Roxy chuckled. "But that wouldn't solve the problem."

"Wait ..." Katherine glanced at me. "Why don't you just do it, then? And why don't other supernaturals know this?"

"Because it's taboo and supposed to be a wolf shifter secret." I glowered at my friend. She had a huge mouth at times. "If you force the change, it's not like vampires. Most don't survive, and the rare few who do end up with some sort of handicap like blindness or deafness. It's like their human body can't handle the magic needed for the transformation so that the wolf is truly part of them."

"Wow, what's the survival rate?" Katherine asked.

"Less than one percent." Wolf shifters were meant to be born, not created.

A car similar to the vampire's caught my eye in the parking lot of an Embassy Suites across the road. "Pull over there."

Egan's tires squealed as he slammed on the brakes.

A horn blared behind us when Egan cut through oncoming traffic.

Lights hit my eyes as a car barreled right toward us. It swerved, trying to slow down.

Our car lurched forward at the last moment, narrowly avoiding a collision. When we pulled into the driveway, I sagged with relief against the door.

"Dude, you almost killed us." Katherine smacked his headrest hard. "What the hell?"

"She told me to turn," he said tightly and pulled into the parking spot behind the vampire's car, "so I turned."

"That's her." Roxy scrolled through her phone and held up an image of the license plate. "See."

"I figured she'd have an apartment or something." Lillith scanned the area. "We try to stay in places where people can't stumble upon our victims, so why in the hell would she be staying in a busy hotel like this?"

"She did leave her victim next to a garbage can." Roxy opened her door. "Maybe she's not concerned."

We followed suit and climbed out of the Jeep.

"No, that still doesn't make sense." Lillith looked inside the car like she might find a clue. "Vampires like sex, so any male victim she finds, she'd want to have kinky feeding sex. The guy would enjoy it at first, but not at the end."

"Is that what she wanted to do with Chad?" I thought she'd only wanted to feed.

"Since she drained the girl first, I'm pretty sure she wanted some fun with him." Lillith shrugged. "That way, she wouldn't drain him too fast before she got her fill of him."

"In both ways, am I right?" Roxy held her fingers like they were guns.

"Really?" Egan looked at her blankly. "You're joking about this?"

Roxy pursed her lips. "Too soon?"

"I'm not sure that comment would ever be appropriate." I loved her, but sometimes, she had a dark sense of humor.

"Nothing seems out of sorts." Katherine focused on the car and then our surroundings.

"Be careful." Egan motioned for us to follow him. "There are a few cameras out here, so we can't come off as shady."

I sniffed the air. "She went in the front." I caught up to Egan as the other three followed behind.

Inside the open lobby, several people were sitting at the bar area. They were all wearing business suits like it was some sort of meeting.

"Speed dating." Katherine motioned to the sign. "She wouldn't ..."

"There are men there looking for a good time." Lillith hurried over to the bar.

"Her smell doesn't go that way," I said low enough so only Egan, Roxy, and Katherine would hear. "It goes this way." I followed the scent to the women's bathroom. However, her scent picked right back up and went down the hall. "Dammit. There's no telling where she is."

"You're right." Egan rushed down the hallway, and the three of us ran after him.

I'd expected her to have gone into a room or upstairs, but she didn't. We tracked her to the very end of the hallway and out the back door.

"What the hell?" Roxy groaned as she walked outside. The warm night air hit us.

"At least, it's only her scent," Egan sighed.

We followed her smell to a parking spot where it vanished.

"Dammit, she's smart." Egan's hands clenched into fists. "She changed vehicles so we wouldn't know what she's driving."

"And a hotel won't tow a car that's been stationary for a few nights." They'd assume it belonged to a guest.

"For her to lose her humanity, that much means she's very old. Which means she is smart at covering her tracks." Katherine placed her hands in her jeans pockets. "That just means we need to be careful, and she won't like that we interfered with that guy from the restaurant. She views him as her target now and will strike again."

"This gets better and better." One thing worked in our favor. "Well, they'll need to hire a new hostess. Maybe I should apply?"

"And work around Donovan?" Roxy shook her head. "Nope, not happening."

"It should be me." Egan straightened his shoulders. "I don't want any of you getting hurt, and she ran when she saw me the other night."

"Well, you are a dragon," Katherine said. "You're the scariest of our kind. One breath of fire, and we're dead."

"It's settled, then." Roxy looped her arm through mine and tugged me back to the hotel bar. "Now, let's go save all those people from Lillith. She likes to think she's got a flowery, charismatic personality, but we know that's wrong."

I forced a laugh. I'd thought going away to college would make my life less complicated, but it sure as hell hadn't.

MONDAY MORNING, my eyes popped open before my alarm went off. I'd been restless all last night since I hadn't come across Donovan at all on Sunday. Before now, I'd seen him every day on campus, but now that I wanted to talk to him, he hadn't shown up once. Nor had Axel.

I gathered a towel and clothes to change into. For whatever reason, I cared more than usual about what to wear. I settled on a pair of dark jeans and a lavender tunic.

"Look at you taking time to consider your outfit." Roxy yawned and threw the covers off her body. "I'm hoping it's not because of a human you'll be seeing today."

"Maybe." I decided not to lie. She'd know the truth regardless. "But don't worry, I'm calling it off today."

"Calling it off ..." She sat upright. "Wait ... did you agree to date him?"

"I'm not saying it was my finest moment." I'd been caught up with him. "But I'll fix it today." I had to. His life depended on it.

"Fine, whatever. But if you don't, I will." She went to her closet. "Let's get going. I'm starving."

We rushed off to the bathroom, ready to start the day.

EGAN WAVED at me as I entered Composition 101. He sat in his usual seat, and I made my way to mine.

"Look who it is," Axel said hatefully. "Did you enjoy the other night?"

There went Axel and me pretending the other person didn't exist. "What the hell does that mean?" Donovan must have told him we'd been together Saturday night.

"If you don't know, that makes it all worse." He scowled at me, dripping animosity. "I warned him about you."

"He invited me there." Donovan wasn't the victim, no matter how badly Axel wanted him to be.

"He must be jealous." Egan waved him off. "Just ignore him. I want to show you something anyway." He held his phone out to me, and I scanned the news article about a dumpster fire and that June had been identified.

It made sense that it had already hit the internet, but I'd hoped it wouldn't get deemed newsworthy. The more publicity it got, the likelier we'd get associated with it.

"What are you doing?" Axel barked. "Showing her nudie pictures?"

Egan's jaw clenched, and he glowered at him. "Don't talk to her like that."

"I can talk to her—"

The professor walked in, cutting off Axel's retort, and started class.

A FEW MINUTES before class ended, I hurried out of the room. I didn't know what the hell was going on with Axel, but he should be pissed at the right person. After all, Donovan had pursued me, not the other way around.

Luckily, footsteps didn't follow after me, so both Axel

and Egan had stayed back in class. They might have more words, but I'd learned that Egan was levelheaded and wouldn't hurt Axel.

I needed a few minutes to gather my thoughts before I saw Donovan again. I had to end it with him, and it caused me physical pain just considering it. My heart felt fractured even though I hadn't even said the words to him.

I hurried to Webster Hall and around to the back. I sat on a small bench right beside the woods, listening to the birds and squirrels running through the forest. If I didn't have class, I'd be out there with them.

When it was only a few minutes before class, I forced myself to stand and head that way. I walked slowly up the stairs, wanting to get there right as the professor entered. I didn't want to chance Donovan figuring out that something was wrong and force my hand. We needed to talk after class.

As I entered the classroom, I found my normal seat vacant with Donovan already next to it, which I'd expected. However, when his eyes landed on mine, he jerked his head away.

Wait, he was avoiding me. Why?

Just like I'd hoped, the professor walked in right behind me, and I didn't get a chance to ask.

I couldn't pay attention in class. I needed to know why Donovan was acting this way toward me.

Right when the professor ended class, I turned to face Donovan. "Can we talk for a minute?"

"Really?" He glared and stood. "You have time for me now?"

"I'm not sure what you mean by that." He radiated the same hostility as Axel. "We spent a large part of Saturday evening together."

"Until you ran off." He headed to the door, turning his back to me.

Oh, hell no. "Hey." I threw my backpack over my shoulder and rushed after him. "I said I wanted to talk." I caught up to him and refrained from smacking him.

"Why were you so late to class?" He kept his gaze forward. "Spending time with that huge-ass guy you left with on Saturday night?"

"Are you jealous of Egan?" I'd never thought of the dragon in any way but platonically.

He didn't answer me and practically ran down all four flights of stairs.

I easily kept pace with him, and when we stepped outside, I grabbed his arm, turning him toward me. "I left with Roxy, Lillith, Katherine, and Egan."

"You let me buy expensive steaks, and to make it worse, you left me to go hang out with him." His face hardened with anger. "What kind of girl does that?"

"You bought their steaks without asking me." He couldn't blame me for this. "And Egan is just a friend."

"Look, it doesn't matter. I feel oddly drawn to you, and this is a huge mistake." He sucked in a breath and straightened his shoulders. "You were right. You've got your large man-friend and some overprotective guard doing your father's bidding. We're not from the same world even if we want to be. I care for you so much, but one of us will get hurt, and I'm not sure who it'll be."

"Are you breaking up with me?" I'd planned to do just that, but this stung worse.

"You can't break up with someone you were never

really with, to begin with." Pain flashed in his eyes as he stepped back. "You made it clear you didn't want to pursue this, and I kept pushing."

"But we're lab partners." I sounded pathetic and needed to stop. This was what I'd planned to do. I had to remember that, but damn, I felt such a tug to him, a lot like the one I'd feel if he was my mate, but that was impossible. He was human.

"We can still be lab partners, just nothing more." He tucked a piece of hair behind my ear.

"I'd give anything for it to be different." I needed him to know I felt the same way. "But I can't risk you getting hurt. My dad ..."

"No, I think I get it." He dropped his hand and smiled sadly. "I'll see you tomorrow."

My wolf howled as I watched him take a piece of my heart with him.

CHAPTER FOURTEEN

"Hey, are you okay?" Egan asked from behind.

No, I wasn't, but no one wanted to hear the truth. "I will be."

"Are you sure?" He stood next to me, his face lined with concern. "You two act like mates. If I didn't know any better, I'd think he was ... your type."

He was being cryptic around the others. "I feel the same way." I hadn't told anyone my suspicions because it felt so damn ridiculous, but he'd confirmed my feelings.

"What do you mean?" He nodded toward the tree line.

That would be a safer spot to have this conversation. "Well ..." I paused, waiting until we'd reached the woods and were out of earshot of the humans. "One time, I could've sworn I saw his eyes glow. Another time, he smelled musky. And the other night, he could make out Roxy in the car across the parking lot when you came looking for the vampire." Tears burned my eyes. It felt like I couldn't breathe.

"What are you two talking about?" Roxy jogged toward

us and stopped when she saw my face. "Oh, girl." She ran over and pulled me into her arms.

"Please, don't." I could barely hold the tears at bay. Her hugging me and making it a huge ordeal would only open the flood gates.

"Okay." She dropped her arms and stepped back. "I told you that you were getting too close. I know it's hard."

"I'm not sure you realize how hard it is." Egan frowned as he watched me. "I think he could be her mate."

Roxy's jaw dropped. "What? That's impossible."

"We were talking about how he seems more than human," Egan explained so I didn't have to. "He looks at her like she's his sun, and she just confided in me several odd occurrences." He filled her in on our conversation.

"Well then ..." she started.

I held up a hand. "It doesn't matter." That was what hurt the most. "Even if he isn't completely human, he isn't completely supernatural either, which means my dad would forbid our relationship."

"But ..." Roxy grimaced, and the salty smell of guilt wafted off her.

"Look, stop." Now that she knew he could be my mate, her story would change. I loved her for it, but it didn't change the fact he wasn't strong enough to meet my father's standards. "Your point is still valid. He and I were on a dangerous path that could only end with my father harming him or worse."

"I still think it's bullshit," Egan said with disgust. "So what? If he's your mate, then he's your other half."

"Maybe ..." I cared about him too much to let anything bad happen to him. "But he's mostly human, and he deserves a chance at a life without the threat of retaliation. I don't need to burden him with our secrets."

Egan adjusted his backpack. "He could still be hunted."

Brock's overly musky smell hit my nose. I lifted my finger to my lips, but it was too late.

Egan continued, "That vampire could attack at any second. She's already killed."

"What vampire?" Brock's nasally voice penetrated my ears. "It can't be the two you're hanging out with. They're soft."

It figured Brock would show up now.

"Some would say they're stronger for not succumbing to their vampire desires," Egan countered, ready to argue.

I'd never seen a supernatural advocate so strongly for those most supernaturals considered weak.

"Oh, please." Brock blew a raspberry. "They're too weak for the power they could embrace. It has nothing to do with strength but fear."

There was no point in arguing with him. "A vampire is attacking people in the area. She drained a girl and left her beside a dumpster. We're trying to make sure our races stay hidden."

"Have you found her?" For once, Brock sounded interested in what I had to say.

"I've seen her." She still made me shiver. "Her skin is translucent, almost like a ghost."

"Damn, then she's old and been around." Brock rubbed his hands together. "I bet she's extremely powerful."

"We aren't here to argue that point," Roxy said with frustration.

"I don't believe I'm talking to you." Brock turned his back to her, facing Egan and me.

"Don't be like that." I always had to broker their relationship. It tired me out most of the time. "Roxy is my friend."

"I know. You remind me all the damn time." Brock pinched the bridge of his nose.

Egan stiffened with rage.

"We have to do something." I cut in before Egan said something to piss him off too. I didn't need my father meddling more than he already was. "She'll get found out with how careless she is."

"Don't worry." Brock straightened his shoulders. "I'll handle it like an alpha heir should."

Ah, there was the dig I'd been expecting. "Who said—"

"Look," he cut in, clearly not interested, "I'll take care of it. I have some resources here that can help me look into it. We won't be found out. Don't worry."

I could at least count on him for that. "Fine."

"I've got to run, but I'll be by later to get you for dinner." He scowled at me. "Since you didn't show up at the game Saturday, I'll fill you in on everything you missed."

Great, that's exactly what I wanted to happen.

THE NEXT THREE weeks all mashed together. If it weren't for classes, I'd never leave my dorm. The more the distance grew between Donovan and me, the more depressed I got. In our classes and lab, he only said as much as he had to, and as soon as the class was over, he'd rush out the door, leaving me behind. If I hadn't been sure before, I was now. He was my fated mate, but that didn't mean a damn thing.

It was now Wednesday night, and Brock insisted on taking me out. His night class had gotten canceled, and he'd said us going out on a date was overdue. I'd initially told him no, but he hadn't left me a choice when he'd threatened my vampire friends.

"You did the right thing." Roxy plopped onto her bed. "I wouldn't want to go out with that prick either, but he would hurt Lillith and Katherine in a heartbeat."

"I mean, what the hell." He had never asked me out before. He was the last person on the planet I'd ever consider going on a date with, yet that was exactly what I was doing. "I'd rather die than spend the evening alone with him."

"You and me both." Roxy rubbed her eyes. "And that's saying something since I've been begging your depressed ass to get out of this dorm. I'm surprised you aren't stinking yet. You still bathe."

That's only because I saw Donovan every day. Even if we couldn't be together, I didn't want to disgust him.

My cell phone rang on my bed, and I inhaled sharply when my dad's name flashed across. "Oh, dear God."

"Let me guess ... Daddy," Roxy mocked.

"You don't think ..."

"It's your father." Roxy leaned back against the wall and dangled her feet off the bed. "Yes. Yes, I do. Just don't answer."

"And have him show up here?" I didn't want to risk him coming here and finding out about Donovan. "Hell no." I answered the phone and kept my voice steady. "Hello?"

"Hello, *dear.*" He only called me that when he was somewhat pleased with me.

"How are you?" If I wasn't overly nice, things would go further south.

"Actually, not as disappointed with you as usual even though it took you too long to agree to spend some alone time with Brock." He tsked. "Brock informed me you're hanging out with the dragon regularly. What information have you found out?"

"Not much." That wasn't a lie. Egan had wanted to confide in me about something the other evening, and I'd brushed it off. I didn't want him to tell me a damn thing. That way, my father couldn't catch me in a lie. "He has a family. That's about all I got."

"They must be planning something, then," Dad said brashly. "Do you think they'll make a power play against me?"

"What? No." Everything I'd learned from Egan told me that he was kind and only worried about keeping our kinds' secret. "He said they're only trying to assimilate in the world again. I don't think they're a threat to your position." It physically hurt to keep my tone even. Dad wasn't fit to rule. He hurt people who got in his way. What kind of good leader did that?

"Well, good." Dad sounded relieved. Maybe I wasn't in trouble after all. "You'd better make sure you put your best foot forward tonight." Dad's disapproval dripped off each word. "We don't need Brock losing interest in you. Their family is wealthy."

"I agreed to one date." Oh, God. Of course, he'd push this. Our little secret was that our family was running low on funds. "Dad, I'm here to study."

"Your duty is to find a strong mate." Dad's voice boomed. "Which Brock is."

"He's a douche." The words fell out before I could stop them.

Roxy's eyes widened, and she burst out laughing. She covered her mouth with her hands, but it was too late.

"Is that girl in there with you?" Dad asked.

"You mean one of your pack members?" I reminded him of this fact all the time. In good packs, alphas took care of their own, but it was obvious ours wasn't a good pack.

"Yes, one of our bottom feeders." Dad scoffed. "A strong pack is only as strong as the strongest. You better remember that."

That's a whole lot of strongs in one sentence, Roxy quipped in my mind.

A smile tugged at the corners of my lips even though I tried to look disapproving.

"Anyway ..." Dad began, dismissing my best friend as usual. "You may be there for an education, but finding a strong mate is more important." He didn't even attempt to listen to me. He was messing with my future, not his own.

"No, I don't want—"

"This is not up for debate!" he yelled. "Brock's family has money and influence, which would align perfectly with our family."

"But I don't want him. This date is a one-time occurrence." I'd done so much for him. I'd gone to all the stupid events and played the part like he expected me to. I never complained. Hell, I'd been too afraid to. He barely tolerated me, and he was the only parent I had since my mom died giving birth to me. I was desperate for his approval, but this was asking too much.

"It's just a date, but there better be more." Dad's voice lowered. "If you don't do this, you can pack up your shit and come home. I won't allow my disobedient child freedom."

If I went home, things would only be worse. He'd make me feel like I was even more of an embarrassment, and any goodwill I had with him would be destroyed. I didn't have a choice. "Fine."

"Good." He paused for a second. "This could all go away if you'd just date the dragon and find everything out."

So there it was. He wanted to dangle coercing Egan into

telling me all of his secrets to control me. "Don't worry, I'll be on time for my date."

"Fine." Dad didn't sound thrilled, but he couldn't do much. I'd called his bluff.

"Okay." There had to be a way out of this. "Is there anything else?"

"Dress nice." He didn't sound as disappointed as I'd hoped. "Remember to behave."

I ended the call. "This is going to be pure hell."

"Yeah, it is." Roxy shivered. "This is like a real nightmare."

"Don't remind me. Better get this over with."

He's going to gloat. Roxy stretched. *And this will only encourage him.*

I had to agree with her. "Then I better disgust him so he doesn't want to go out with me a second time."

She smirked. "Are you, dear friend, hoping to sabotage your date?"

"Maybe." Since my father was forcing me to date this asshole, it was only right that I take matters into my own hands. "But surely not on purpose."

"What are you thinking?" Roxy rubbed her hands together with a devilish expression. "Bad hair, bad makeup, horrible ensemble, or a combination of all three?"

"Nope." I had to at least look the part. If he took a picture of me looking out of sorts and showed my dad, it would be hell on Earth. "I have to look like perfection." Everything else had to fall apart.

"Look?" Roxy lifted her brows. "Not act?"

"Exactly." The smile on my face hurt. I'd never tried to disobey or disappoint my father before, but my future hung on the line. I had to disgust the asshole so he'd never want to take me out again. That shouldn't be too hard since an alpha desired a perfect princess.

CHAPTER FIFTEEN

"There." Roxy pointed to the mirror. "We're all done."

She had insisted on doing my makeup and helping me pick out my outfit. I had to look the part so Dad wouldn't completely lose his shit on me. I needed to be smart about this.

My eyeshadow was a dark gray, and she'd painted my lips a medium pink. My pink hair had been curled into loose waves that hit my shoulders. She'd done amazing, and the look was exactly what I'd been going for. "Thanks."

I stood and ran my hands down my lacy black dress. The dress hugged my body and flared slightly past my waist. If my dad could see me, he'd give me a nod of approval. I never got more than that. No praise or anything, just a nod indicating he wouldn't nag me—yet.

"You look gorgeous." Roxy placed the brush back on the nightstand. "Where are you two going?"

"No clue." He lived in the dorms too, so I didn't have to worry about going back to his place alone. Worse case, I could link with Roxy and get her ass there to save me.

"I'm sure it'll be pretentious just like him." Roxy leaned her head back. "I wish I could help."

"Don't worry." I waved my hand over my face and body. "This is more than enough."

"What are these plans of yours?" Her face lit up. "I wish I could be there to watch."

"I'm not sure yet." I would have to make my plan as the night went on. "I'll go with the moment and my gut."

She chuckled right as there was a knock on the door.

I didn't want to do this. *Satan is already at the door.*

Roxy headed to the door and glanced at the clock. *He's right on time, the eager son of a bitch.*

She opened the door, and Brock stood there with a light pink gift bag. He waltzed into the room without invitation and headed straight to me.

He looked more ostentatious than normal. He was dressed in black slacks, a lavender button-down, and a black jacket. He wore a dark purple tie. On anyone else, it would be hot, but not on him. It confirmed that he was Lucifer's son in my mind. Well, maybe that was insulting the son.

"Here." He held the gift out to me. "I figured now that we've finally officially begun dating, you might enjoy this."

Roxy leaned against the door, watching.

Not sure what to expect, I pulled the white tissue paper from the bag and found a picture frame inside. *What the hell?*

What is it?

I'm not sure. I pulled the frame out and almost burst out laughing. It was a picture of him in a tuxedo on the back porch of his house. He attempted a sultry look, but he looked more constipated than anything else. *Oh my God. No.* "Um ... thanks?" Why on Earth would he think I'd want this?

"You're welcome." He tugged at his tie and smirked. "I figured we'd wind up together this year, so I had that made for you."

Roxy rushed beside me, and her eyes almost bulged out of her head. "You realize flowers are usually good first-date gifts?"

"A picture lasts a lifetime." He looked down his nose at her. "This is a gift that won't die, and she can look at it every morning."

Do we really want to wake up to that nightmare? she asked with such hate.

Nope, don't worry. If I could throw it away, I would. *We'll put it face down and pour salt all over it and around it. It should keep the demon at bay.*

"You look perfect, as you should." He nodded, reminding me of my father.

I wasn't even sure how to respond to that, so I didn't. "Are we ready?" The sooner we got out the door, the quicker I could return. Or so I hoped.

"Oh, yes." He smiled. "I love that you're eager." He took my hand and led me to the door.

Have fun. Roxy laughed loudly in my mind.

Kiss my ass. I couldn't believe she enjoyed seeing me in pain.

We walked to the parking lot and headed to a newer BMW parked in the back.

"Whose is this?" When we'd arrived here, he'd picked us up and had a driver. I'd assumed he didn't have a vehicle.

"It's mine." He didn't bother opening my door but rather went to his door and slipped inside.

There went him being a gentleman, which didn't surprise me. I got settled into the vehicle, and he pulled out.

"When I informed my dad that I'd be taking you out, he

had someone drop the car off." He pulled onto the main road. "Besides, it sucked not having a way to get around. I'm not riding that bus anymore to away games. Those humans are too annoying."

"You won't blend in taking your car." That was the point, to mix.

"Like I give a fuck about that." He rolled his eyes and scoffed. "We're meant to stand out from them."

Yeah, I refused to engage with him on this topic. "Where are we going?"

"There's a decent steak house around here."

My stomach dropped. "I'm not in the mood for steak."

I hoped we weren't going where I thought we were.

"Well, I am," he snapped. "So that's where we're going. Haynes Steakhouse has decent reviews, and it's not too upscale where people will find us being there odd."

Wow, this date had started off with a bang. There was no getting out of it, and my stomach dropped. Both Egan and Donovan worked tonight. I only knew about Donovan from Egan. It wasn't like he told me a damn thing anymore.

All too soon, we were parking outside the restaurant.

The urge to refuse to get out of the car consumed me, but I forced myself outside. I knew I should at least look like I'd tried on our date.

We entered the main lobby and found several couples waiting. Brock marched to the front and said condescendingly, "Brock Roberts, table for two."

"If you—" The hostess started, but Brock didn't let her finish.

"I have a reservation." He glowered at her.

"I ..." She flinched and grabbed two menus. "I was ... going to say, follow me to the table."

God, he was more of an ass than I'd realized. We

already made humans uncomfortable, so we didn't need to throw our weight around like that.

As we walked past the tables in the front, I searched for Egan and Donovan. This was ridiculous. I shouldn't feel guilty about being on a date. Donovan was the one who'd called it off, not me. But that didn't matter. It still felt like I was cheating.

Egan's powerful presence came from the kitchen, and he stopped dead in his tracks. "Sadie? Why are you ..."

Brock appeared and took my hand in his. "Hello, Egan."

"You're here with him?" Egan asked in horror.

"Well, I've been backed up and figured a good steak would work it all out." I patted my stomach.

"What?" Brock's hand stiffened, and his nose wrinkled. "Are you being serious?"

"Hey, a girl's gotta do what a girl's gotta do." I wanted to die of embarrassment, which meant I was on the right track.

"Uh ..." The hostess's voice quavered. "This way."

"Come on." Brock yanked me forward, and I glanced over my shoulder at Egan, mouthing, "Help me."

His golden eyes turned to slits for a second, and he nodded and returned to the kitchen.

"Donovan will be your server today." The hostess placed the menus on the table and stepped back. "He'll be with you shortly."

Oh, fuck me. It had to be him. "Are you sure we should stay here?"

"Even more so after running into Egan." Brock slid into the seat and pointed at me to sit down.

Jackass. I had a funny feeling I'd be cursing most of the night. As I went to sit down, an epiphany hit me. I slid into the seat and stopped myself short, falling on my ass. My legs shot upward so my panties were on full display.

"Sadie, what the hell?" Brock barked but didn't budge to help me.

I flailed around, hoping I never saw any of these people again in my entire life. Of course, that was when I heard *his* voice.

"Hey," Donovan said as he ran over and bent down, wrapping an arm around my waist. "Are you okay?"

He wasn't supposed to have seen this. That woke me up enough to pull my skirt back over my legs. "Yeah, I tripped on my high heels."

"Get your hands off my date," Brock snapped.

"Maybe if you'd helped her up, you wouldn't be having this problem." Donovan held his ground as he assisted me to my feet.

No, he couldn't challenge Brock like this. This was why he and I couldn't be together. "No, it's fine." I stepped away from Donovan, needing to break the tension between the two men. "I just got tangled up in my heels."

"Dear God, Sadie." Brock frowned. "You're more graceful than this. You're stomping around like a cow."

"Don't—" Donovan began, but I clapped my hands loudly.

"I would love a Long Island Iced Tea." I needed all the liquor to get me through the night. "And the largest steak you got, medium-rare." It took a lot of liquor to get a shifter buzzed without wolfsbane, but I was down for the challenge.

Donovan glanced at me. "You're not—"

"I'll get it," Egan called from a few feet away. "Don't worry about it, man."

"I'll take a glass of water." Brock scowled at me. "And the same type of steak as her."

"Yeah ... okay." Donovan didn't seem to want to leave, but he slowly walked off.

Brock settled into his seat. "Why haven't you been to any of my football games?"

I'd bet telling him it was due to him being on the team wouldn't go over too well. "Studying and the like. But I heard you guys are killing it this year."

"Thanks to me." He puffed out his chest. "I've been an amazing quarterback. Perhaps the best they've ever had. If I was like the others, I could sleep with so many women. Sometimes, my position is such a burden."

He was on a date with me, telling me he wished he could sleep with other women. Classy. I needed that drink and fast.

Egan appeared at my side with it. "Here you go."

I took the tall glass from him and grabbed his arm when he tried to leave. I sucked the entire drink down in one long gulp. Egan and Donovan stared at me.

"Another, please." I handed the glass back to Egan. "Might as well keep 'em coming."

"Sadie, this isn't ladylike," Brock chastised.

"Don't worry." Egan winked at me. "I got you." He returned to the bar to get me another.

"Here's your water." Donovan set the glass of water on the table, but he glanced at me with worry.

Nope. He didn't get to do that. He'd left me. Pushing away any self-respect, I let out the longest burp I'd ever had in my entire life.

The table beside us stared, and Brock went still. His face turned a shade of pink.

"I'll go ..." Donovan smashed his lips together and stepped back. "... check on your steaks."

"What in the hell are you doing?" Brock breathed

rapidly, his nostrils flaring. "Are you trying to embarrass me?"

"I'm embarrassing you?" I feigned shock. "What am I doing?"

"Your father trained you better." He leaned over the table and spoke low, "Get your shit together."

That wouldn't happen.

We sat in silence, staring each other down. This was worse than I'd expected.

Egan appeared again with two glasses. "Here you go."

"Thanks." I took the first one and drank it down in one long gulp again. I locked eyes with Brock and let out another huge burp.

If my asshole father thought Brock could control me, he'd be learning differently tonight. I might be an obedient daughter, but I was quickly getting over that too. If Donovan and Axel could be here on their own merit, dammit, I could work hard and make it happen for me too.

"Sadie ..." he growled as I took my other drink and sipped on it.

I wasn't sure how long we sat there, locked in a dominance war. I refused to avert my eyes just as he was determined not to lose to a woman.

The smell of steak hit my nose as Donovan's familiar footsteps headed our way.

Donovan laid the first steak in front of me and placed the second one in front of Brock. "Does everything look good?" Anger laced his voice.

"Look isn't the problem." Brock grabbed his silverware and cut a piece off. "Is this a joke?" His voice rose a little higher than necessary.

"I'm not sure what you mean?" Donovan's jaw clenched as he stared the awful alpha heir down.

"Does this look medium-rare to you?" Brock turned his plate to show that the meat had no pink in it whatsoever. "Or are you that stupid?"

"I thought you said medium well." The rotten stench of lies wafted off Donovan.

He had no clue we knew he was lying. He had a good poker face, so if it hadn't been for the smell, I wouldn't have known.

"Sadie, check yours," Brock ordered.

I did what any graceful lady would do. I grabbed my fork and stabbed the steak right in the center. I already knew mine was cooked right; the smell was delicious. Instead of cutting a piece off, I lifted the whole steak and bit into it over and over. Once I got a piece in my mouth, I chewed with my mouth wide open. "*Mns gdd.*"

"Stop eating like that right now." Brock's eyes glowed as he tried to force the alpha will on me.

But it wouldn't work. "No." I stared him right in the eyes and bit off another piece. The juices flew across the table and hit his face.

I refused to cower any longer.

CHAPTER SIXTEEN

Donovan laughed beside me, and Brock's face turned the shade of a ripe tomato.

"Stop it right now," Brock rasped.

My wolf growled inside me. Neither of us liked being talked to like this. Why had it taken until now for us to find our courage?

I squared my shoulders and took a huge bite of my steak, but this time, I jerked my head from side to side, thrashing the meat with my canines.

"What would your father say if he knew how you're acting?" He leaned back in his seat.

That threat might have worked a month ago. "You could call him." I took my phone from my purse and slid it across the table to him. "You can even use my phone."

He flinched, not expecting it. "Fine." He, for once, didn't seem so sure of himself.

"Should I dial his number for you?" Wavering was off the table. I would never bow to this jackass again.

"Wow, it's sad that you can't fight your own battles."

Donovan grabbed Brock's plate and shook his head in displeasure. "You have to call your date's dad to tattle?"

"You know nothing," Brock snarled. "Why don't you go fix my fucking order and leave me to handle my bitch."

"Do not call her that." Donovan dropped the plate on the table. It landed with a thud right in front of Brock, and the steak bounced, causing the juices to land on his lavender shirt. Now it had wet spots that almost matched his tie.

Brock clenched his hands and climbed to his feet. "You stupid—"

Egan appeared out of thin air. "Is there a problem here?"

"Yes." Brock stuck a shaky pointer finger at Donovan. "He's being disrespectful, and I need to see the manager."

"No." Egan crossed his arms and hovered over Brock. "You're making a scene, which isn't tolerable. I'd hate for it to get back to your family."

Brock turned his attention to me. "These are the people you want to surround yourself with?"

"Egan is a great friend." I left out Donovan for his protection. The more I focused on Egan and my vampire friends, the better. "And he would never force my hand. Come on, you called my dad to make sure I couldn't backout on this date, as if threatening my friends wasn't enough."

"You listen here." He pushed Egan out of the way and got in my face. "Get it through your stupid head; you will be mine." He grabbed my arm, squeezing it.

"No, I won't." I wouldn't let this egomaniac bully me.

"Let her go." Donovan's eyes glowed faintly as he reared back to punch Brock.

Before he could land it, Egan snagged his arm and pulled him away.

"If you don't release her and leave, there will be a problem," Egan promised as he moved in front of Donovan. A small trickle of smoke left the corner of his mouth as he stared Brock down. "Do I make myself clear?"

Brock's grip slackened, but he didn't remove his hand. "This is none of your concern."

His meaning was clear—this was a wolf shifter spat, and Egan was interfering.

In general, supernaturals minded their own business when it came to the problems of other species.

"She's my friend," Egan said low and threateningly. "So, it is my business. It's best if you leave before things get out of hand."

"Fine." Brock dropped his hand and stepped back so he could look at me without his back to Egan. "We will pick this up later. You will be mine, and I'll be aligned with your father." He spun on his heel, leaving me behind and not bothering to take care of the tab.

At least, he had the balls to finally admit why he wanted me.

"Hey, are you okay?" Donovan asked, voice full of concern.

"Yeah, I'm fine." If Egan hadn't been here, everything would've gotten worse. Hell, it was clear that things weren't over yet. He'd only walked away because of Egan and the restaurant full of humans.

"I'm going to take an early break." Egan turned to Donovan. "And take her home."

"No, I can Uber." I didn't need Egan getting in trouble. We needed him here in case the vampire came back for Chad. "Don't worry about it."

"Nope, you're my closest friend here." Egan's face softened. "I'll make sure you get back to your dorm without that asshole causing you more problems."

I hadn't considered that. "Okay." I felt bad taking him up on it, but he was right. I wasn't in the right frame of mind to fight Brock alone. I hadn't realized I was willing to confront him until we'd gotten here and I'd seen Donovan. Maybe I needed to resign myself to a life of being alone. I wasn't interested in being with anyone but him.

"I'll be right back." Egan hurried off toward the kitchen.

Donovan's fingers brushed where Brock had grabbed my arm. "Are you okay?"

"Huh?" I hadn't registered the pain until now. "Yeah, I'm fine." It surprised me that the handprint still marred my skin. By tomorrow afternoon, the bruising would be gone.

"That asshole deserves to get his ass handed to him." Donovan scowled, though his eyes were full of concern. "He can't treat you like this."

Whatever barrier he'd put between us was gone, but he'd slam it back up soon. As he should. This thing between us couldn't happen. "No, it's fine."

"You should tell your dad." He stared at my face, waiting for my reaction.

"No, it's useless." If Dad found out, he'd take Brock's side, but Brock wouldn't tell him. If he did, it would look like he couldn't handle being an alpha, so I had that in my favor. "Just don't worry about it. Your concern will only get us back to square one."

"Would that be so bad?" he asked in barely a whisper.

"You were right." I had to put a stop to this moment of tenderness. He only felt it because he'd seen Brock manhandling me. "Let's just end this before we get caught up in the moment." If he pushed this, I wouldn't be able to say no.

"Sadie?" Egan called from the hallway that led to the front of the restaurant. "Let's go. I need to hurry back."

"Okay." Thankfully, Egan had saved me from whatever potential problem Donovan and I had been about to create. I glanced at Donovan, and my hand touched his arm of its own accord. Damn traitor. "I'll see you tomorrow." I forced my legs forward despite my heart and wolf screaming at me to stay. The longer we were here, the more of an epic mess we'd create.

"Yeah, okay." Donovan nibbled on his bottom lip and turned to watch me leave.

The moment I stepped next to Egan, Donovan said, "Sadie?"

I paused. I worked to get my heart under control before I looked at him. When my strength found me, I spun around before I lost it again. "Yeah?"

"Be careful." He blew out a breath. "And call if you need me. I'll always be there for you."

My brain couldn't form a response since everything inside me told me to close the distance between us. "Thanks." Wow, what a meaningful response.

"Come on." Egan gently patted my arm.

It was enough to bring me back down to Earth. "I'll see you." I turned around and followed Egan to the door.

Outside, I scanned the area to make sure no vampire was near. "Are you sure this is a smart idea?"

"Yeah, I'll be back within fifteen minutes, and I told Chad to call me if she pops back up." Egan headed to his Jeep and opened the door for me.

I couldn't hold back my laughter.

His brows furrowed. "What's so funny?"

"You're my friend, and you just opened the door for

me." I slid into the passenger seat. "Brock didn't even bother doing it, and we were supposed to be on a date."

"He's a self-absorbed asshole." Egan handed me a bag I hadn't noticed he was carrying and shut the door. Within seconds, he entered his side. "What else do you expect? Not all men treat ladies like they should."

It would have been simpler if I felt for him the way I did for Donovan. My dad would approve, and he was such a good guy. But neither of us was interested in the other. That was the thing about shifters: you could always tell when someone was attracted to you. "Very true. Whoever you end up with will be one lucky girl."

"I can say the same about you." He started the car and pulled onto the main road.

The smell coming from the bag hit my nose. "Is that your dinner?"

"Nope, yours and Roxy's. I had the kitchen prepare you two a meal while I took care of the ticket." Egan focused on the road. "You won't need to leave your dorm tonight after I drop you off."

"Shit, I need to pay for dinner and this." Money hadn't even crossed my mind.

Egan patted my arm. "I took care of it."

"Thank you." I'd found better friends here than back home, except for Roxy. She had been the only person in my corner until now.

"You do realize that Donovan definitely has a wolf in him. I saw his eyes earlier. It may be faint, but it's there."

"Yeah, I know." Did he think that made a difference? "But he's mostly human and can't shift. My dad would never allow it."

"So what?" Egan faced me. "Your dad shouldn't dictate your entire life. If you let him, you and Donovan will be miserable. He's wolf enough that he can't let you go. You two are fated mates."

"Don't you think I know that?" I snapped and regretted it. He was trying to help, but I'd grown up obeying my dad without question, which now made me so damn mad. I'd always known my father was wrong. "I'm sorry."

"No, it's okay." He turned into the university and frowned. "Growing up with your father couldn't have been easy. I know you're struggling, but even though humans don't have magic, that doesn't make them worthless. They survive in this world without speed, strength, or supernatural hearing. If you think about it, they're more resilient than we are."

"How can you stick up for them?" I'd tried to understand, but I couldn't get there. Even though I agreed with him, humans had hunted dragons down to near extinction.

"Not every rumor is true, you know?" Egan pulled up to the sidewalk and parked his car. "Humans get painted as monsters by our kind out of convenience."

"What are you saying?"

"Nothing." He opened his door and exited the car.

I followed suit, grabbed the food, and met him on the sidewalk. "No, really."

"Now isn't the time to have this discussion." Egan motioned for me to follow him. "I better get back."

"You're right." I hurried and caught up to him. "Did I get you into trouble?"

"Actually, the manager is cool. He saw what happened and was more than willing to allow me to take you home."

Brock's obnoxious scent hit me hard. I scanned the area but didn't find him anywhere. The closer we got to the building, the more his scent dissipated, so he hadn't entered the dorm.

"The prick was waiting on you." Egan opened the door to the girls' dorm and waved me in. "I figured he would be. He wanted to pick a fight with you alone."

"I'm not surprised." I entered the building and gave him a hug. "He probably won't bug me again tonight since you walked me in. Thank you."

"Not a problem." He returned the embrace and dropped his arms. "Go on. I'll stay here until you get into the elevator."

"See you tomorrow at lunch." We'd all been eating together for lunch and most dinners. The only time I didn't eat with Egan, Lillith, and Katherine was on the two nights Brock expected to eat with Roxy and me. Though he only actually wanted to eat with me, I never wanted to be alone with him, so I dragged her along. Tonight had proved that my gut was right.

When I got to my floor, I took a moment to collect myself before seeing Roxy. She'd want to know every sordid detail.

I walked into the communal bathroom and heard someone sniffling. Something had to be wrong. I turned toward the line of bathroom sinks against the wall and found a petite girl with long, teal-colored hair. Her skin had a golden-pink hue, and despite her crying, she was drop-dead gorgeous. Her eyes were almost the same color as her hair.

"Are you okay?" Normally, I felt awkward, but her presence was rather calming.

"Uh ..." She startled and wiped the tears from under her eyes. "Yeah—I mean, no." She turned toward me and tilted her head. "You know how they can be."

That's when it hit me. She was fae. They rarely came to

this realm. "Who?" I sniffed the air and scanned the room. We were the only two in here. "Humans?"

"Yeah. A few girls invited me to hang out and proceeded to make fun of me." Her voice sounded melodic like a bell. She sniffled. "My parents were right about me coming here."

"Hey." I walked over and gently touched her arm. As soon as our skin touched, my head grew dizzy, and something sizzled inside me. "It'll be okay," I said breathlessly, shocked by our connection.

She narrowed her eyes at me but didn't remove my hand. "What kind of supernatural are you?"

"I'm a wolf shifter." I forced a smile. I'd thought fae were more in tune with stuff than that.

"Interesting ..."

"Naida," a girl called, and footsteps squeaked into the bathroom. A human girl entered and looked at the fae. "I'm so sorry about all of that. I was hoping maybe you wanted to go back to my room and hang out."

"Yeah, that sounds good." The fae smiled and took a step in her friend's direction, but she paused and glanced over her shoulder. "It was nice to meet you."

"I agree." It relieved me that one of the girls had come here to make things right. It proved that humans weren't all bad. "Have a good night."

I watched the two leave and realized that the longer I put this off, the more questions Roxy would have.

A few minutes later, I stepped into the dorm room and found Lillith and Katherine hanging out. The two vampires sat on my bed while Roxy was sprawled out on hers. They were watching a movie.

Katherine lifted a brow. "You're back early."

"Not soon enough." I placed the bag on my desk and

pulled out the two boxes. I headed over to Roxy's bed and smacked her legs. "Move."

"Ugh, fine." She sat and took the box from me. "But only because you brought me food."

Lillith paused the movie. "How did it go?"

"Not great." I picked the steak up with my fingers, not worried about making a mess. After the scenes I'd caused tonight, eating with my hands in my dorm room didn't make me flinch.

Roxy smirked. "Care to elaborate?"

I filled them in on everything.

"Oh, my God." Roxy stopped eating and blinked. "Who are you?"

"I don't know anymore." I'd hoped for a bit of freedom here, but I was finding so much more than that. "But the asshole actually expects me to continue dating him."

And that was the problem. He hadn't even considered that I might put up a fight. That's how far gone I'd been ... until now.

"Well, I'm glad you've found a backbone." Roxy began eating again. "Your dad is an asshole who does shady shit everywhere."

"Don't remind me." My mind was already over thinking about Dad and Brock and was solely back on Donovan.

My phone buzzed, and dad's name flashed on the caller ID. "I've got to take this." I sucked in a deep breath and answered, "Hello?"

"I heard the dragon interrupted your date." My dad didn't sound angry.

"Uh ... yeah." Egan hadn't interrupted it, but I wouldn't correct him and say that I'd ruined it.

"Well, Brock is very upset." Dad tsked. "But for once, I'm proud of you."

"What for?" He used to always get angry when I made Brock mad. None of this made sense.

"For capturing the dragon's attention," Dad said proudly. "I almost thought you didn't have it in you."

I remained silent, not sure how to respond. I wanted to cry in relief, though, since Brock was focusing on Egan and not Donovan. Egan could protect himself.

"Now I need you to find out all his secrets and where the other dragons are staying." Dad chuckled darkly. "I'll be there this weekend for homecoming. It'll be nice to meet him. Invite him to dinner with us, will you?"

Anxiety coursed through me. My dad coming here would only cause more problems.

CHAPTER SEVENTEEN

I tossed and turned, unable to fall asleep. Between Dad and Brock, I felt like I was suffocating. I sat up in bed and glanced at my phone. It was close to midnight, and a run sounded good. It would help me destress so I could sleep the rest of the night.

To avoid disturbing Roxy, I took my time climbing out of bed and slowly opened our door. Once in the hallway, I relaxed. Roxy was a grouchy bitch when her sleep got disrupted.

The buzz of televisions and conversations spattered through the dorms, but it sounded like most people were asleep. I took the elevator, and soon, I stepped outside and inhaled. Just being outside calmed me.

My phone buzzed in my pocket, and I pulled it out to see a text from Egan.

Did the asshole bother you again?

I loved that Egan had deemed Brock too unworthy for a name. **No, but my dad called. So I had the pleasure of dealing with that.**

He texted back. **Wanna meet up?**

A friend to talk to would be nice. **Sure. I'm already in front of the girls' dorm.**

Be there soon.

I placed my phone back in my pocket and paced in front of the building as I waited. I soon spotted a towering figure heading my way.

"Hey," Egan said as he approached me.

It was funny. I'd never seen him in anything other than business-casual clothing, so to see him in sweatpants and a t-shirt comforted me. "Hey, yourself."

"I figured you'd be up." Egan stopped a foot away. "It was a long night for you."

"That's why I can't sleep." I looked up at the almost full moon. I wanted to ask about Donovan, but I couldn't be that forward. "I can't turn my brain off. Did anything happen when you got back?"

"You mean, did Donovan say anything?" He lifted a brow, calling me out.

"Fine, yes." I blew out a short breath and shifted my weight to one side. I hated how well this dragon had gotten to know me in less than two months. "And did you get into trouble? I do worry about you as well."

"I was fine, and nothing horrible happened while I was gone." Egan smirked as he tapped his chin. "And did Donovan work tonight? I can't remember." He teased, pretending that we all hadn't been together at the restaurant just hours ago.

"Really?" He'd called me out, so I might as well own up to it. "You're enjoying torturing me. Haven't I been through enough for one night?"

"Fine." He gestured for us to head toward the library. "Let's walk and talk."

"Okay." He must have needed to get out into nature too.

"Donovan was torn up," Egan said as we walked slowly to the woods. "He wanted to call you."

"But he didn't." That was one thing that had kept me up —wondering why he hadn't reached out to me. He'd seemed so damn concerned.

"Because he deleted your phone number from his phone after you all ended things." Egan's face scrunched. "But you really didn't end anything because your mate bond connection is already partially there."

That burned. "Why did he do that?" I shouldn't have been hurt. I'd come very close to doing the same thing to him. Having his number in my contacts made it too easy to swipe his name and text or call him. The only reason I hadn't was because it would have made it too final, which apparently, he was okay with.

"To not call you at night." Egan pointed at me. "He begged me for your number, but I refused. I'm not getting in the middle of you two."

Donovan wanting my number again warmed my cold heart. It shouldn't have. Nothing had changed. If anything, things were worse. Brock would want to get even and force me to be with him. "You did the right thing. It's more impor-tant than ever to fight our bond."

"You see, that's where I disagree." Egan stiffened, ready to fight.

"Look, I don't want to discuss that right now." I needed to be straight up with him. "It's rare that we get to talk alone."

"Okay ..." He tensed.

"My dad is coming here on Saturday, and he wants you

to go to dinner with us." We'd reached the woods, so I stopped and faced him. "It would be smart of you not to go."

"Really?" Egan rocked on his feet. "Won't that cause more issues for you?"

"It will." There was no point in lying. He'd know. "But my dad wants to learn all about you, and I wouldn't recommend it."

Something shifted in his eyes. "Why is that?"

"Because my dad isn't a good man." I couldn't believe what I was saying, but Egan deserved to know the truth. "He wants to be in charge of all the races, and he'll do whatever it takes to get there. That's why I never ask you questions because I can't risk my dad finding anything out about you. And neither one of us needs that."

"I gathered that." Egan entered the woods. "And I'm glad I wasn't wrong about you."

"What does that mean?" I followed behind him, and as soon as I stepped into the woods, a calm settled over me. Being outdoors made me feel connected to nature and my animal.

"You never pushed for information from me, which I found odd, even more so when I realized who your dad is." He took a worn trail. "I'm glad you're different. You honestly are my closest friend here, with the rest of your girl posse taking up the next spots."

"Yeah, we have a good group of friends." The five of us were working together, and it felt effortless. "But one day, I do want to understand why you're so protective of humans."

"Maybe." He chuckled. "But right now, you need to get your head on straight and make things right with Donovan."

"You know I can't." He made it sound so simple. It wasn't.

"I find it odd that you think you're stronger than fate."

Egan didn't even bother to look at me. He continued his trek deeper into the woods.

His words struck me hard, but I had no other option. If I bowed to fate, Donovan would die.

———

I WAITED until the last possible second before entering biology. I wasn't sure whether I'd find a solemn, concerned, or uninterested Donovan. The past several weeks, I'd grown to expect an aloof one, but after last night, I was scared, wondering what to expect.

Class started in a minute, so I entered in a hurry. My eyes landed on him immediately.

He'd been watching the door.

As I approached, his body relaxed. He said, "Are you okay?"

Okay, concern was the obvious winner. "Yeah, I'm good." I sat and pulled my books out of my bag. I needed to say something. He'd witnessed my train wreck last night. "And I'm sorry about everything."

"Which part?" He met my gaze. "Coming to the restaurant on a date with a douchebag, or me having to watch Egan take care of you?"

So he wasn't concerned; he was pissed. I wasn't sure if that was better or worse. "Both." I tapped my fingers on the table. "All of it."

Luckily, the professor walked in, effectively cutting off the entire awkward conversation.

———

As soon as the lab was over, I threw my stuff back into my backpack and stood. I needed to get out of here before he hurt me more than he already had. I deserved it, but I was keeping my distance for his sake.

"Hey." Donovan took my arm before I could walk away. "I need to talk to you."

"I think we said everything we needed to."

"No." He kept a firm grip on me as though I might run away. "Please. I just want to talk."

He deserved that. "Fine, but only a few minutes."

"Come on." He dropped his hand and walked out of the classroom. He led me down the stairs and to the back of the building, which opened up to the woods.

No one was back here since most students stayed toward the front. He entered the woods, which surprised me.

Once we were surrounded by trees, he stopped and turned to me. He sucked in a shaky breath. "There are a ton of things I don't like."

Wow. I hadn't expected this. "Please don't. It'll kill me." I'd never begged for something before, but hearing how much he hated me ... I couldn't bear it. "I'm sorry about everything. My dad pressured me into that date last night, and I had no clue where we were going until we'd left. I even tried to get him to go somewhere else, but he refused. I didn't mean to make a scene, embarrass you, or get you into trouble."

He lifted a brow and tilted his head. "Are you done?"

"Yeah." I turned on my heel, ready to leave. Maybe I'd need to drop biology. I couldn't be around him like this.

He must have expected my reaction because he stepped in front of me, blocking my path.

"It's my turn." He crossed his arms, ready to fight me over it.

"Fine." Maybe this was what I needed. "Tell me everything you hate about me."

He stepped toward me and narrowed his eyes. "I hate how you tore down my defenses the very first time I laid eyes on you."

I straightened my back, and my eyes met his. It would be all downhill from here, and I wouldn't submit to anyone anymore.

"I hate how when you're not near me, I feel like I'm going insane." He lowered his head ever so slightly, and his nostrils flared. "And I hate how I pushed you away when all I want to do is have you near."

My breathing hitched. He needed to get to the nasty part fast before I crumbled at his feet.

"And I despise how you felt like you had to go out with that asshole last night when it was clear you didn't want to be there." His eyes took on the faint glow of his wolf surging forward.

"Was it that obvious?" A smile broke through even if I hadn't meant for it to.

He lowered his head even more, and his minty breath hit my face. "If that's how you act on a date, I need to take you on a proper one."

"What?" I whispered.

"See, you're not letting me finish." He tucked a piece of hair behind my ear. "And I hated that I wasn't the one who took care of you and brought you back to your dorm. I refuse to make that mistake again. I'm done fighting this."

"But ..." I started, but he placed his finger to my lips.

"Don't." He cupped my cheek. "I'm done. I can't anymore. Not after seeing you with him."

"You just said you knew I didn't want to be there." I needed to step away, but my traitorous legs stayed stuck in place.

"That's the only reason I didn't lose my shit." He stared at my lips.

They tingled now because of it. "But Axel—"

"He'll get over it." He lowered his lips to mine.

The buzzing between us intensified. If I'd thought our bond had been strong before, it was nothing compared to this moment. His soft tongue flicked against my mouth, begging for entrance.

I had to keep my head on straight. There was so much at stake. I pulled back. "One of us will get hurt. I can't have that on my conscience." I hated to do this, but I had to be strong. If I succumbed to this, Donovan would be dead as soon as Brock or my dad picked up on what was going on. I licked my lips once more, trying to remember his taste, and I turned to run.

"Sadie!" he called out.

"I'm sorry." I pushed my legs hard, needing to get away before I turned back to him. *Roxy, call Egan. Tell him to come out in the woods and make sure Donovan stays safe.*

He's on his way. Roxy's concern hit me hard. *What's wrong?*

I didn't have the energy to tell her right this second. I ran toward the library, staying in the woods. I needed to shift and now.

I found two thick bushes where I could shift and hide my clothes. I hurriedly changed and ran toward the forest.

Sadie, where are you? Roxy connected with me, clearly annoyed.

I had to get away and go for a run. The trees flashed past me as I connected to nature and the ground all around me. I found myself running back toward Donovan. I needed to make sure Egan got to him and he was protected. He could be in danger with the crazy vampire around.

As I rounded the corner, I found Donovan and Egan.

"I can't be here without her." Donovan ran his hands through his hair. "I thought we were finally on the same page, and she rambled on about her father, and me getting hurt if he found out about us."

"Look, she'll come around." Egan frowned, and his head turned in my direction. "She feels the same way about you as you do her."

No, he wasn't supposed to be encouraging Donovan. I would kick his ass when we were alone.

"Then why is she fighting it so hard?" Donovan looked crushed.

"Because she thinks she's protecting you." Egan patted him on the shoulder. "But she doesn't realize you two are weaker apart." Egan's eyes locked on mine. "You two are meant for each other. Everyone can tell. That's why Roxy and Axel are scared about you connecting. They don't want you two broken beyond repair, but what they fail to see is that it's too late."

"Wow, thanks, man," Donovan grumbled as the two of them walked back toward civilization. "Way to make it even more depressing."

"Don't worry." Egan tugged on his arm. "You two will get together. I'll make sure of it."

That conniving dragon, but I couldn't stay mad. He knew we were fated mates, and he was trying to be a friend.

A branch broke behind me, and I spun around, looking for the source. It was too loud to be from an animal, which meant I wasn't alone.

CHAPTER EIGHTEEN

A s I followed the sound, the overly sweet smell of a vampire hit my nose. The overwhelming smell was stronger than those of my vampire friends, which meant this was someone older and stronger. *Roxy.* I hated to bother her, but I might need backup.

She linked back immediately. *What's wrong?*

The fact that she was hiding behind the university didn't sit well with me. I hunkered to the ground and growled at her.

"I wouldn't do that if I were you." The vampire chuckled. "I have information you might want."

If she thought that would work, she'd soon learn differently. I stalked toward her, and she bared her teeth, her canines dropping.

"Go shift so we can talk," she commanded. "I need to tell you something about your little guard."

She had to mean Brock. I was probably stupid for listening to her, but I was intrigued. If she knew something and I could get her to spill it before I killed her, it could benefit us. I connected back with Roxy, *Nothing. False alarm.* I needed to find out whatever I could before calling for back up.

Facing her, I stepped back, and when I was far enough away so she couldn't attack me, I ran to where my clothes were and changed quickly. I was back in minutes despite Roxy's constant nagging. My best friend knew something was up, but I ignored her.

The sun was high, so how in the hell was she even out here? "What could you possibly want to tell me?"

"I wouldn't say want."

I found her in the shadow of three large trees.

She had on a long-sleeved hoodie and pants despite the heat. And despite her dreary appearance, she was gorgeous, a trait of any supernatural, but especially a vampire. They needed to lure in humans even though everything inside the human screamed at them to run. Her eyes were a dark red, revealing her gluttonous appetite.

How had we not known about all of her kills? "I'm sure the information will come at a price."

"Of course," she said as she smirked, giving me chills.

I had a feeling the price was one I wouldn't be willing to pay. "I'm not interested." I turned on my heel, ready to march away.

"Even if it's about your daddy?" she cooed.

This had to be a trap, but my feet stopped.

"I figured that would get your attention." She sounded so arrogant. "Besides, you shifted and came back, so you are curious."

"Isn't it foolish for a vampire to come out at the peak of daylight hours?" I could easily attack her and put her in the sunlight.

"Maybe ..." She tilted her head, examining me. "But I have backup in case things don't pan out."

"What do you mean?" My ears pounded with anxiety.

"I can't tell you all my secrets." She bobbed her head. "But if something happens to me, Brock will retaliate. He knows the dragon is after me."

"Brock ..." That skeezy son of a bitch. "You're working with him." We'd told him about her to get his help, not so he'd fucking recruit her.

"I've already given you more than you deserve." She lifted a hand, revealing the gun in her grasp.

"Whoa." I stepped back. "You're here to kill me? I don't think Dad would be too thrilled about that."

"I'm not so sure." Her shoulders shook with laughter. "But don't worry, I'm not here to kill you—yet."

That wasn't as comforting as she thought. "What do you want?"

Dammit, Sadie. Roxy's anger flowed through our bond. *What the hell is wrong, and where are you? That wasn't a false alarm.*

The vampire's here. That probably wasn't the best way to calm her down. *But I need a minute. She wants something from me.*

Yeah, your blood, Roxy quipped back. *Get the hell away from her.*

Vampires don't like supernatural blood. Not for survival. Only human blood sustained them. They might drink their mate's blood during sex, but it was more for pleasure than necessity. *I'm in the woods near where Egan and Donovan were, but don't come out here yet.*

Her freaky-ass eyes landed on me. "To give you information for something quite small."

"Which is?"

"That delicious-looking boy I tried to drain last month before you interfered." She licked her lips. "That stupid dragon always works the same nights he does, and I'm tired of waiting."

We figured this would happen, and we'd been hoping she'd get reckless. However, we didn't have this in mind. "No."

"It's just one human." She rolled her eyes. "What's the big deal?"

"Well, for starters, you're sloppy." I pointed at her. "You left June on the ground."

"Next to the dumpster." She shrugged her arms. "The humans only needed to put her in it. I don't see the big deal."

"The big deal is that you were sloppy, and the humans would've found your bite marks." Her humanity had completely left the building, confirming our suspicions.

"Humans are stupid." She waved her free hand and lowered the gun slightly. "They'd explain it away as some sort of dog attack or something like that."

She was insane. "Not if you're racking up bodies all around town. You're being careless."

"Well, if you give him to me, I'll make sure to dispose of him properly." She rocked back on her feet. "There won't be a problem."

I'd never felt any contempt or hate toward humans, but ever since coming to Kortright, I'd felt protective of them. Maybe it was Donovan's fault or Egan's influence, but humans shouldn't be treated like they were nothing. "Chad is a friend, and we aren't handing him over." A friend was a stretch, but she didn't need to know that.

"Friends with a human." She sounded shocked, but it soon vanished. "I shouldn't be surprised since you're in love with one."

No, she couldn't know that. "I don't know what you're talking about." The air around me smelled rotten.

"Wow, that's a big lie." She exaggerated waving her hand in front of her nose. "You forget that vampires have excellent hearing, and I was already in the woods, waiting for you to leave that building." She gestured to Webster Hall.

Great. The day Donovan had decided to come clean and wanted me back was the same day she'd been waiting for me. "How did you know I'd come into the woods?"

"I didn't." She pointed to her outfit. "But I figured if you saw someone dressed like me in the woods, it would catch your attention. I didn't know a human would pledge his love and devotion to a wolf. It's strange, though. The dragon wants you two together."

"We're trying to be careful." I wracked my brain for a way out of this. "We don't want to alert him to our race."

"Do you think I'm an idiot?" she asked with annoyance. "Your telling him that you don't want him wouldn't make him suspicious of supernaturals, but I'm sure Tyler would find it interesting that the two of you are hanging out and getting caught up in human business."

"Why don't you tell him and find out for yourself?" I said, calling her bluff. I wouldn't stand around and let her threaten me.

We're all here. Roxy linked back with me. *We're coming in.*

Don't. I was being stupid, but I needed to keep her talking. *She's telling me stuff. I'll let you know if it changes.*

Sadie, she growled, but I ignored her.

"Listen here, bring me that boy or I'll kill your little human friend." All humor vanished from the vampire, and she scowled at me. "I'm tired of this little game. It's growing old."

"No." I would fight her right here and now. I didn't give a shit that she had a gun. "I won't bow to your demands."

"How about this ..." She stepped into the sun, but her clothing protected her from the rays. "If you bring me the guy, I won't attack anyone else here on campus."

"But you haven't been." I hadn't heard about anyone else disappearing in the woods.

"Oh, I have." She grinned evilly. "You see, someone may be helping me cover my tracks. Maybe they could help me lure in your delicious little human friend. He would have a good time before I drained him completely."

The sexual innuendo rang clearly. My wolf surged forward. "You will not touch him."

"Hmm ... interesting." She pointed the gun right at me. "Your wolf is protective of him too. Then I'm sure Tyler wouldn't have a problem with this." Her finger squeezed the trigger.

She's about to shoot me. I'd been so stupid to keep them at bay.

Dammit, Sadie! Roxy roared through our bond.

A gunshot pierced the air, and the bullet headed straight for my heart. Surprisingly, my eyes locked on the bullet, and something pulsed from inside my stomach, making me dizzy. It slammed into the bullet, slowing its speed. I dropped to my knees, and the bullet brushed past my hair, narrowly missing me.

"How the hell?" the vampire yelled as she pointed the gun at me once more.

Footsteps pounded toward us as my friends came to my aid. I should have told them to stay back, but it wouldn't have done any good. They would've heard the shot.

Are you okay? Roxy asked as her auburn wolf landed next to me. She placed her nose in my face and then my chest, sniffing for blood.

"I'm fine."

Egan bounded through the trees, heading straight for the vampire.

She hissed and pointed the gun at him. "Stay back."

He ignored her, and she fired at him.

Green scaly wings ripped Egan's shirt in two, and they flapped, lifting him into the air. The bullet missed.

"No." The vampire dropped her arm, turned, and ran deeper into the woods.

Egan landed and retracted his wings.

"You can half shift?" I hadn't expected that. Only some of the strongest shifters could control their shift.

"Yes." He jerked his thumb in the vampire's direction. "Let's go get her before she gets away."

"We'll go this way." Lillith pointed to the right. "That way, if she changes directions, one of us should catch her."

"I'll go with them." If they split up from Roxy and me, they might not be able to call for help. Roxy and I could use our pack bond. "You two stick together." I stared at Egan, hoping he'd pick up on me asking him to protect my best friend. I didn't want to verbally ask and make my friend feel inferior, but Egan was stronger than her. Hell, he was stronger than me.

He nodded, which allowed some of my stress to melt away.

"Come on." I grabbed the vampires' arms and tugged them with me. "Let's head her off before she gets too far." I called to my wolf, letting my clothes rip in two.

I sniffed the air and took off after the vampire. We expected her to run as hard as she could, which probably meant she wouldn't. If I were out to hurt someone, I'd try to split them up and divert their attention.

The vampires ran slightly behind me, scanning the area while I let my nose guide me. We tapped into our senses to make sure she didn't sneak up on us.

No animals roamed the area, so she couldn't be far ahead. Creatures could sense the evil in her. Her sweet smell covered the rotten stench inside her.

Something off filled my nose. It smelled of sweet dirt as if she were trying to hide her stench. I slowed, catching Katherine's and Lillith's attention.

"What's—" Katherine started, but Lillith covered her mouth with her hand.

Lillith placed a finger to her lips, telling her friend to be quiet.

I moved slowly, careful not to make a noise. I looked behind me and jerked my head, telling them to stay in place.

Somehow, they understood me. I wouldn't question it at the moment.

The scent came from a few low-hanging bushes between the trees. The closer I got, the sweeter the air smelled.

I connected with Roxy, not wanting to do anything else stupid. *I think I found her.*

I'd almost gotten killed earlier and didn't want a repeat performance. I might not be so lucky a second time.

Okay, we'll cut over and meet you there.

Refusing to lose my trail on her, I inched closer and closer. I was standing ten feet away when something leaped out of the bushes at me.

Long fangs extended, the vampire bitch lunged straight at my neck. Before her teeth had the chance to dig in, I dropped. I lifted my forelegs, hitting her legs so they flew over her head. She landed hard on her back.

Katherine and Lillith descended on her. Lillith yanked the hoodie off her head, and the old vampire screeched in pain. The enemy vampire elbowed Katherine in the head. Her body went slack and slid to the ground.

The older vampire grabbed Lillith's head and kneed her in the nose. Lillith crumbled to the ground, shrieking as she pinched her nose to stop the bleeding. If vampires lost any blood, they struggled since it nourished their bodies. That was one reason they needed regular feedings.

I lunged at her, but she stumbled back and held the gun right at my face. I swiped my claws out, cutting into her arm.

"Agh!" she yelled, and her jaw clenched. She sped toward me and grabbed the fur around my neck, trying to pick me up with her injured arm.

I jerked my head toward her hand and sank my teeth into her injury. I thrashed to tear her skin open.

She shoved me back, and I stumbled several yards away.

"You'll pay for this," she snarled. "I'll get both humans. Just you wait and see." She fired the gun at my leg, but this time, nothing poured out of me, and I couldn't move away fast enough. I crumpled and howled in pain.

CHAPTER NINETEEN

The vampire ran away, actually looking to escape this time. She seemed nervous, but I wasn't sure why. She'd taken three of us down without breaking a sweat.

I slowly climbed to my feet and tried going after the bitch, but pain radiated through my leg, which had me limping. There was no way I could catch up to her.

The pounding of paws and the flapping of wings alerted me that Egan and Roxy were getting close. But they were too late.

She'd gotten away. Again.

We're almost there, Roxy connected with me. *Is she still there?*

No. Even through my mind, I growled. Tears sprang to my eyes now that I had split my concentration.

Egan appeared, still in half shift. His dragon eyes scanned the area for the enemy. When he looked at me and the vampires, he swooped down toward us. "Are you okay?"

"Does it look like we are?" Lillith hissed as she pinched the bridge of her nose. "My nose is broken, and Sadie got shot in the leg."

Roxy ran straight to me and shrieked, *You got shot in the leg and didn't tell me?*

In my defense, it only happened moments ago, and I've been preoccupied. I tried not being a complete ass. She was upset and concerned. *And you were already on your way. Are you telling me you weren't getting here as fast as possible?*

She lifted her wolf head up and blew out her nose. *Fine. Point proven.*

If I hadn't been hurt, I would've cracked up. She reminded me of a horse.

"What happened to her?" Egan walked over to Katherine and brushed the hair out of her face.

"Elbow to the head." Lillith groaned and rocked back and forth. "I need blood to heal so I can take care of Sadie."

"First things first." He gently patted Katherine's face. "We need her to wake up, get those two some clothes, and get you some blood."

"I can get there." Lillith stood, and blood trickled from her nose.

"You probably shouldn't." Egan gestured to her blood-soaked shirt. "You might scare them."

Most humans didn't like to be around blood.

A small moan left Katherine, and her eyelids fluttered.

"She's coming to," Egan whispered as he scanned her head. "She's got a decent knot hidden by her hair."

Katherine inhaled sharply, and her eyes opened. She scooted out of Egan's hands.

"Hey, it's okay," Egan said softly. "The vampire is gone."

Roxy sat and watched them. *Is it just me, or are you surprised at how gentle a dragon can be?*

We'd been told that dragons were vicious and self-centered. Either Egan had broken the mold or what we'd heard was wrong. I leaned toward the last option, especially after his warning of people painting others as monsters. Now, I questioned everything Dad had told me. *Yes, I am. But I have a feeling most of the dragons are like him.*

Yeah, I think you're right. She sniffed my leg. *The bullet is still in there.*

That's what I'd been afraid of, and now it hurt even worse because she'd told me that. *Can we stop talking about it?*

"We need to get them help." Katherine stood on shaky legs, but her attention fell on both Lillith and me. "They're injured."

"We know." Egan held his hands out, expecting her to topple over. "I'm hoping you can go grab the wolves a change of clothes and some blood for Lillith."

"I can do that." She took a few slow, strong steps, and her body relaxed some. "I'll be right back."

"Be careful," Lillith said, sounding nasally. "Call me or yell if you need our help."

"The vampire's long gone." Egan frowned. "Which is probably for the best since all of you are hurt."

"Okay, I'll be back." Katherine took off running back toward campus at vampire speed, her figure a blur.

"Let's take a look at your leg." Egan approached me slowly like I was a rabid dog. He gently lowered his hand toward my leg. "I'll barely touch it."

A low growl emanated from my throat. I'd thought he was strange for acting that way, but my wolf was reacting to his dragon. She was scared he might hurt us, and we had no good way of protecting ourselves right now.

"I promise." He continued reaching for me. "I won't hurt you."

Lillith marched over and stood next to him. "She's not healing."

"No, she used silver bullets." Egan frowned and rubbed a hand down his face. "She had every intention of shooting her."

That comforted me so much. Granted, I had dodged the kill shot. I had to appreciate the pain. It meant I was alive.

"I need to get it out of her." Egan lowered his head, ignoring my warning snarls.

"You better wait until she's back in human form." Lillith glanced at me. "Her animal is at the forefront and about to attack you."

"Shifting will hurt like a bitch though." He grimaced, and concern lined his forehead.

"Yeah, but if you don't," Lillith pressed, "she'll fight you and wind up more hurt."

Can you hold her back? Roxy lay beside me, trying to calm my wolf down.

No, she's scared. Hell, both my human and wolf sides were scared. They weren't exclusive of each other, which made this whole situation even worse.

The four of us stood in silence for a few more minutes before we heard Katherine returning. She'd made good time.

She stepped into view and looked right at Roxy and me. "You'll have to reassure the RA that I had permission to go into your room. She kicked me out and tried taking your clothes back, but I promised you both knew about it." An outfit hung on each arm, and she held two containers of what had to be blood out to Lillith, along with my cell phone.

Thank God she'd found it.

Roxy nodded in response.

In a flash, Lillith took both cups from her and downed one in a matter of seconds.

"Okay, here you go." Katherine laid Roxy's outfit in front of her and held mine. "Sadie, I can help you get dressed if you'd like."

I shook my head. My leg might be injured, but I could still move my arms and legs. I got to my feet again, not putting any weight on my right rear paw. This would be a slow and steady process, but I didn't want any help.

"Let me know if you change your mind." She held my clothes out to me.

It was hard being in wolf form and unable to communicate to anyone but Roxy. I put the clothes in my mouth and headed toward the trees that the vampire had hidden in. Roxy followed close behind like a threat could pop out at any second.

Even though she wasn't strong by wolf definition, she was fierce where it counted. We got settled, and I lay down on the ground. I dreaded this because it would hurt, but Lillith was right. To heal, I had to shift, or else I'd bleed out.

I closed my eyes and pulled my wolf back inside me. She struggled and protested, which was unusual, but she didn't want to retreat in case a threat still loomed. Being injured made our animal side go wild.

Pulling all of the strength I could find, I yanked her back. My fur rippled, making my injury move and tug. My stomach roiled as pain took hold.

Dammit, if it was already this bad, I feared what the next few minutes would be like. Despite every ounce of my body protesting, I jerked my wolf in more. My bones broke, and I threw my head back, and a loud and painful howl left me.

I needed to be quiet and not alarm any nearby humans,

but the pain was too unbearable ... too excruciating. My skin stretched and molded as my body shifted from being on all fours to two legs.

My skin ripped at the bullet site, making a loud, terrible sound I'd never forget. My howl morphed into a scream as my human form took hold.

"Sadie." Roxy fell to her knees next to me, naked as a jaybird from her shift, and her eyes widened in horror. "Egan, get your ass over here."

I was completely naked, but it was the furthest thing from my mind. I just needed the pain to recede.

Egan barreled into the bushes, and Roxy stumbled back, grabbing her clothes and retreating to dress. Lillith and Katherine were only a few steps behind him.

He settled at my feet, keeping his eyes focused on only the injured part of my leg. "Okay," he rasped. "This will hurt like hell, but the longer the bullet's in there, the worse it'll be."

"Just ..." I grunted almost incomprehensibly. "... do it."

He shoved his fingers into the bullet hole, and blinding, white-hot pain slammed into me. I thought I'd been in pain before, but I'd been wrong. This was so much worse. I couldn't imagine what a bullet wound to the heart or head would feel like. Hell, maybe instant death would be better than this.

His fingers twisted into my leg, searching for the bullet.

It hurt so bad I couldn't breathe. My vision went black, and I welcomed the darkness, but it wouldn't take hold.

"Dammit, Egan," Roxy growled. "You better get it out before I kick your ass."

"This isn't fun for me either." He closed his eyes as he felt his way inside my body. "I feel it. Just bear with me a little longer."

I wasn't sure how much more I could take. He pushed his fingers deeper, and a raw scream spilled from me. My wolf surged forward, but we were too damn weak to shift again.

"I got it." He pulled his fingers from the hole and held the bullet in the air. "It's over."

But the pain hadn't vanished or even barely receded.

"Someone help her!" Roxy yelled as tears fell down her cheeks. "She's hurting."

"Here." Katherine moved beside me and was about to bite into her wrist.

"No, let me." Lillith came to my other side. "My blood is older and stronger."

"But you've already lost so much," Katherine said with concern.

"I'll be fine." Lillith bit into her wrist and lowered it to my mouth. "Take some. It'll help you heal quickly."

I considered refusing. Drinking vampire blood didn't sound appealing, but I was desperate. I opened my mouth, ready for any kind of relief.

As her blood dripped over my tongue, I was shocked that it didn't taste anything like I'd expected. Normally, blood had a metallic hint to it, but not hers. It tasted like rocky road ice cream. The exact flavor. Who would've known? At that moment, I understood why some people got addicted to it.

I grabbed her arm and held it to my mouth, taking deep sips.

"Whoa." Lillith grabbed my hair and yanked my head back. "Easy girl. Don't drain me. I get that you're injured, but I lost a lot of blood. You've had plenty."

I snapped back to reality, and my pain began to subside. I slowly sat upright and watched as the torn skin mended back together. A scab formed, and almost all of the pain had disappeared. "Holy shit." I wasn't sure what else to say.

"I couldn't agree more." Roxy blinked and sat back. "I understood that vampire blood healed, but I had no clue how much so."

"I've been around for a while." Lillith wiped the excess blood from her wrist on her blood-soaked shirt.

"Okay." Egan stood and looked awkwardly away. "I'll leave while she gets dressed." He rushed out of the woods, without glancing once.

"Do you think he's gay or a virgin?" Roxy tapped her finger against her chin. "What kind of college-aged guy acts like that? Most men would have been examining Sadie like she was their favorite type of chocolate. Their tongues would be hitting the side of their face or something."

"Or he could have manners." Katherine shook her head and sighed. "There are still some gentlemen out there."

"Really?" Lillith shrugged. "I kind of agree with Roxy."

"You all know I can still hear you," Egan complained. "I'm not even ten feet away."

"Your point?" Roxy winked at me.

"Is it even worth a response?" He groaned. "I was being respectful."

"Give me a second." I got to my feet and almost cried in relief. If the pain hadn't been haunting my mind, I'd have thought I'd imagined it all. I grabbed my clothes and dressed, ready to get the hell out of the woods. It normally was my reprieve, but right now, I wanted distance from it.

Within minutes, the five of us were heading back to campus.

"You do realize something cuter would've been appreciated." Roxy looked at the Kortright sweatshirt and jean shorts Katherine had gotten her. "If a cute guy sees me in this, I might die."

"Oh, please." Roxy enjoyed the dramatics at times. "You don't need to worry about human cute boys, and secondly, that is a standard outfit most college girls wear."

"I," she said, flipping her long red hair over her shoulder, "am not most college girls."

"Don't we know." Lillith snickered.

"Oh, kiss my ass, hussy." Roxy tried to hide her smile as she lifted her head high.

"Did the vampire say anything to you before she left?" Egan asked, effectively diverting the conversation.

"Just that she is going after both Donovan and Chad." I'd been trying to protect Donovan, yet he was at risk just the same.

"I hate to tell you this, but you'll have to babysit Donovan tonight." Egan glanced at me, a grin on his face. "I've got to work tonight and can't call in seeing as Chad will be there."

"One of them can do it." I pointed to the vampires and Roxy. "I can't be with him. You know why." He wanted us to be together, but that couldn't happen.

"And why can't you?" Roxy lifted a brow. "He's your fated mate."

"He's part wolf, isn't he?" Lillith kept her eyes forward. "I had a feeling he was."

"He is," Roxy said. "That's why it's pointless."

"Because it doesn't change anything." He was still weak in my dad's eyes. Having some wolf in him wouldn't elevate him in shifter society.

"It changes everything." Roxy sighed. *If he's your mate, you have to be with him.*

"Then, it's agreed." Egan looked at me. "Roxy will come

with me to the restaurant and help keep an eye out for the vampire, and the vampires will keep watch tonight around the dorms."

I ignored Roxy's comment. "And what exactly am I supposed to do? Stalk the woods?"

Egan stared at me as if in a dare. "You're going to go eat dinner with him and keep an eye on him until I get home from work."

"No ..." I couldn't.

"Do you want him to get hurt?" Egan asked. "He only trusts you and Axel, and his best friend can't protect him. Hell, they could both wind up hurt. Besides, what's the point in fighting when he's already at risk?"

"Here." Katherine handed me my phone.

His words settled hard, and I took the phone. They were right. The vampire knew something was up between us, so I should protect him.

I pulled up his contact and sent him a text message.

Can we hang out tonight and talk?

This wasn't smart. It was a very bad idea. My heart knew I couldn't deny him any longer.

CHAPTER TWENTY

I stood alone in my dorm room, my heart pounding. I wiped my sweaty palms on my jean shorts and stared at my reflection in the mirror. My nerves were shot. Whether I liked it or not, eating with Donovan tonight would change everything between us. He wanted me, and dammit, I wanted him.

Normally, I'd want Roxy in my corner, but it was for the best that she was off with Egan. She'd be making comments that I wouldn't want to hear.

The clock was mocking me. It had to be. I had five minutes before I needed to leave and meet him at the Student Center. Time had flown yet gone slow. My heart and head warred with each other, but it didn't matter. I had to make sure he stayed safe. I couldn't live with myself otherwise.

You're so emotional. I can feel you from here. Roxy's voice popped into my head. *It'll be okay.*

I'm not so sure. I looked at my leg. The long scar was still visible and looked like a battle wound. I realized that I should wear jeans so people wouldn't look at me like I was crazy, even if it would be healed in the next hour or so. I could still feel the vampire blood in my system as it centered around the wound site.

Moving the hangers in the closet, I came across a pair of light-wash jeans that would work with my dark university shirt. I removed the pants from the hanger and put them on slowly and methodically, ensuring that I didn't bother the wound.

Now that I was situated, it was time to meet him. It felt like this was my first time being around a guy I truly liked. Yeah, I'd done things with other guys in the past, but this felt new.

I pushed away the thoughts and headed out the door. There was no point in getting all worked up.

I approached the Student Center, and Donovan stood outside, waiting for me even though it drizzled. His gaze landed on me, and my body warmed. If a look could do that, I might combust if anything more ever happened between us.

My breath caught as I said, "Hey."

"I should've known there was a reason you were hanging outside," Axel said with disgust. "What the hell are we waiting on her for?"

He hadn't come alone. I didn't blame him, but it stung. I'd been both looking forward to and dreading alone time with him, and he had no intentions of actually doing that.

"Don't talk to her that way," Donovan growled. "You insisted on coming even when I told you I didn't want you to."

"Because I figured it had something to do with her." Axel sounded hurt, but he focused all that energy on me. "Haven't you done enough?"

I deserved the hate. "I'm done hurting him." The words had left my lips before I could tamp them down.

Hope sprung into Donovan's eyes.

"Oh, because that makes it all better." Axel spat on the ground. "Now you want him? Or just for tonight."

"Leave her alone." Donovan faced his friend. "I get that we've been the only stable relationship in each other's lives, and she won't change that. It can't be the two of us forever."

"Is that what you think this is about?" Axel's mouth dropped. "That's not it. I don't want to see her ruin you."

"It's not your choice." Donovan stepped toward his friend. "I know you don't like it, but it's my choice. I can't walk away and always wonder, 'What if?' That might destroy me."

The already crumbling wall around my heart fractured even more. Neither one of us would be able to come out of this unscathed whether we stayed together or left one another. It was the sort of situation that held no good outcomes.

"Fine." Axel backed up and threw his hands up. "You've already made your decision, but don't come crying to me when she tramples you." Axel stalked away from him and walked straight up to me. His eyes took on a small hint of a glow, which I hadn't expected. He lowered his voice to barely a whisper. "If you break him, I'll break you. I don't give a flying fuck that you're a girl."

I opened my mouth to respond, but Axel wasn't interested. He marched back toward the dorms without a backward glance.

"Hey, I'm sorry about him." Donovan took a hesitant step toward me. "He's my best friend and trying to protect me."

"No, I get it." I was glad he had a fiercely loyal friend.

Those were hard to come by, and I had a feeling they'd grown so close because they sensed each other's wolves. "It's a good thing. You're lucky."

"Roxy seems just as fierce." He placed his hands in his pockets as awkwardness hung between us.

This wasn't how it was supposed to go.

A group of people brushed past us and entered the building while talking about homecoming, which was in just a few days.

"Ready to eat?" Donovan asked and opened the door for me.

My stomach gurgled in response. Kill me now.

"I'll take that as a yes." He chuckled and motioned to the door. "Ladies first." He chewed on his bottom lip, looking so damn adorable.

"Thanks." I breezed past him, focused on food. I needed a distraction from whatever brewed between us.

Inside, I waited for him to catch up. The place was packed, and I couldn't see an open booth or table. "We might have to go eat somewhere else."

"We could eat outside at one of the benches." Donovan walked so close to me that our arms were brushing.

That would be ideal, but I didn't want to be out in the open, especially if the vampire was watching. "In the drizzling rain? Maybe, we could go to my dorm." Wow, that sounded sexually charged even though I hadn't meant for it to.

"What about Roxy?" he asked as he led the way to the cafeteria.

He didn't know where she was. It'd sound weird if I told him she was hanging out at the restaurant. "She's gone for the evening."

"Okay then." He glanced at me from the corner of his eye.

My stomach trembled. I hadn't expected him to say yes. "I'm going to grab a burger." I hurried away, needing to get my head on straight.

The line moved way too fast, and soon, I stood outside the cafeteria, waiting on him. I placed my tray down on the condiments table and pulled out my phone. I pulled up the group chat for the five of us. **Anyone see anything out of the ordinary?**

Lillith responded within seconds. **All good out here for now but stay out of sight as much as possible. She's old, which means she's very strong and fast.**

We'd learned that earlier today. I hadn't understood what it meant that the older a vampire was, the more powerful they were, until I'd seen her take the three of us down today. My father hadn't really encouraged me to train as a child, saying I was a weak female, but it was clear he'd put me at a disadvantage. I should be able to protect myself and not rely on some stupid male. Our society was so antiquated, yet we cast stones at humans for the very same traits.

We're eating in our dorm. All the tables were taken. I winced, waiting on the reply.

He may be your mate but remember to put a rubber on. Roxy texted back instantly. **No babies until you're out of college.**

And there was the response I'd expected. I wasn't sure whether I preferred this or her telling me I needed to stop seeing him. Either way, it unsettled me.

"Are you okay?" Donovan's voice pulled my attention to

him. His forehead creased with worry as he strolled over to me.

"Yeah, just Roxy being herself."

"Is she on her way home?" Donovan glanced at the tables again, looking for a vacant one.

"No." I shook my head. "She was just checking in."

"Oh ..." He laughed. "You ready to go?"

He had four slices of pizza, a chicken sandwich, and fries on his tray. He had the appetite of a shifter.

"Hungry?" I had to give him hell after what he'd said to me that one day. "No wonder you were worried that I might eat more than one burger. Then, there wouldn't have been enough left over for you."

"I deserved that." He walked toward the door. "And I was being an ass. I'm sorry for that. I just felt a tug toward you, and it scared me."

He deserved to know the truth, but I wasn't sure how to tell him about our kind. If I were human, I probably wouldn't want to hear the scary truth—that monsters were real.

"I understand. Believe me." We'd been feeling and experiencing the same things.

As we approached the doors, they opened, and Brock came strolling through. He stopped when he saw Donovan and me together. "What's going on here?"

I wanted to say "school project," but that would hurt Donovan. I was at a loss as to how to explain this away.

"Sadie and I are hanging out together." Donovan lifted his chin and stared the alpha heir down.

"Hanging out?" Brock tilted his head back and looked at me. "Is that true?"

"Yeah." I wanted to avert my gaze, but that would make me look as if I were submitting or ashamed. I wasn't doing anything truly wrong. Dad and he considered associating with weaklings wrong. However, if I didn't stand behind Donovan, it would undo our progress.

"What would your father say?" Brock placed his feet a shoulders' width apart. He wanted to make sure I knew it was a threat.

"You're pathetic enough to bring her father into this?" Disapproval dripped from Donovan's words. "It's sad when you know that's the only way to get her interested in you."

"Do not speak to me," Brock said a little too loudly in front of humans. "You aren't worth it."

"Stop." I couldn't let this escalate any further. I had to keep Donovan next to me. Yes, having him around thrilled me, but dammit, it was also necessary for his survival. I dropped my voice so low it was barely audible as I said, "Part of your future as alpha is knowing how to handle things without making a scene."

He snarled, "Do you think I don't know that?"

"Sure doesn't seem like it." I stepped into his bubble and almost bumped noses with him. I couldn't back down. Whether Dad and he liked it or not, I was an alpha heir too. "You're making a scene."

Brock's soulless eyes glowed as his wolf surged forward. He didn't like being challenged. "You better be careful what your next actions and words are. I'd hate for things to get bad for you."

"I'm not trying to challenge you." I really wasn't. I just wanted him to leave me the hell alone and mind his own business. I wasn't asking for much. "I want you to stop acting like you own me."

He barked out a laugh. "Oh, don't worry. I'll own every inch of you." He stepped away and motioned me toward the door. "Go enjoy your last night of freedom."

His words chilled me. He surely wouldn't tattle on me to my father, would he? Either way, it didn't matter. I wouldn't be intimidated by him, not anymore.

"Come on, Donovan." I shoved my shoulder into Brock as I passed him.

"Stop threatening her," Donovan rasped as he passed.

"Enjoy your night." Brock chuckled. "It may be your last."

Not only was he potentially working with the vampire, but I feared he could tell Dad everything. If he did, the little showdown wouldn't change much. She'd probably already informed him of what she'd witnessed in the woods. After all, she had to prove her loyalty.

Donovan stepped next to me, and we walked the entire way back to my dorm in silence.

I wasn't sure what to expect when we entered the room, but as he shut the door behind me, I kept my back to him. I didn't want to see his face.

"What does he have over you?" he asked, and I heard him set the tray down on my desk.

"Nothing." I winced. That wasn't completely true. He deserved to know. "My dad isn't the best guy."

"Oh, don't worry." He got closer behind me. "I already gathered that."

I placed my tray on Roxy's desk and turned around. I braced myself to find disgust on his face, but instead, I found concern and, dare I say, love. No, he needed to be scared. That was the normal reaction. "You could equate him to the mob or mafia. If anyone goes against him, he has them killed or worse."

He laughed but stopped short. "You aren't kidding, are you?"

"No, that's why I keep pushing you away." I touched his

cheek with my fingertips. "Being with me is risky. You deserve to be happy."

"But I can't be happy without you." He placed his hand over my fingers, holding them to his face. "Something deep in my soul is connected to you." With his free hand, he rubbed his eye. "God, that sounds so cheesy, but it's true. I want to be with you, no matter the risks."

"I feel it too." I needed him to know that. "And that's why I need to protect you. To make sure you stay alive. You can find someone else—"

His lips touched mine, cutting off my words. He pulled back and stared me right in the eyes. "I don't want anyone else, and dammit, I get a say in this."

"But—" I began, but his lips were on mine once more.

His tongue swooped in between my lips, and his familiar taste invaded my senses. He wrapped his arms around my body and pulled me flush against him. Each stroke of his tongue drove me and my wolf wild.

I responded in earnest, needing him. Dear God, I'd never wanted anyone like this before. I moaned in pleasure, and he picked me up and laid me gently on the bed.

My hands snuck under his shirt and traced his rock-hard abs.

His body quivered on top of mine. "Damn, that feels so good." He lifted me up, removed my shirt, and discarded it on the floor.

I needed to stop him, but before I could protest, he unfastened my bra and tossed it on the foot of the bed.

"Donovan ..." I begged, but I wasn't sure why. I didn't want him to stop, but I hadn't told him everything yet.

"I love it when you say my name." He placed his mouth on my breast and flicked the nipple with his tongue.

My body burst into flames, needing him in all ways. "Oh, God."

The little bit of encouragement was all he'd needed to unfasten my jeans and slip his hand between my legs. He rubbed in the right spot, making me nearly come unglued right there.

I shoved my hands down his jeans and touched his hardened, huge length. Every inch of him was sexy.

He moved his hands and sat back, yanking my pants and panties off. Then, he removed his jeans and boxers.

My eyes took in every square inch of him, and I was ready for all of him. I leaned forward, pulling his shirt from his body. Once he was naked, I took the time to scan him from head to toe.

"You're gorgeous," he rasped, his eyes glowing. He lowered his arms around my head and positioned himself between my legs.

My body was ready, but my heart and head both yelled at me. "Wait. There's something you need to know before we continue."

"No, I want you." He kissed my lips. "Nothing will ever change that."

I had to get it out before I did something I regretted. "I'm a wolf shifter."

"What?" he asked. "Are you kidding?"

"No, and you're part wolf too." I placed my hand on his heart, enjoying his touch before he left and never wanted to see me again.

CHAPTER TWENTY-ONE

"Are you serious?" Donovan stayed where he was, but his eyes widened. "You're saying you're a wolf, and I kind of am too?"

"Yes, I'm sorry." I should've said something before now, but I couldn't have us complete the mate bond without him knowing what he was doing. "If we have sex, our bond will be sealed. There will definitely be no turning back."

He licked his lips. "Our bond?"

"The reason you feel connected to me is because we're fated mates." I could only imagine what this sounded like to him. "We are two halves of the same soul."

"You're saying we're meant to be together?" A grin peeked through.

"Fate wants us to be with each other." I cupped his cheek with my hand. "But you can still choose."

"If we do this ..." He chuckled. "Have sex, that is ... we'll be bound for the rest of our lives?"

"We will." If being a wolf didn't scare him, this probably would. From everything I'd seen, young men got spooked when talking about commitment. "It'll be awful to be apart for too long."

"Then I'm in." He kissed my palm. "I don't know what this means, but this crazy explanation kind of makes sense between us. And honestly, I know I want you forever, so if this will make it happen, I'm all on board. We can handle the wolf part later."

"Maybe you need more time to think it through." My wolf growled in my head but didn't fight me. We needed to take care of our mate and make sure he was okay with everything between us.

"Do you have any reservations; other than the ones you've already addressed?" He looked at me, seeing into my soul. "You've been fighting this more than anyone."

"Because I didn't want to trap you." I hadn't realized it until now, but that was the truth. I wanted to protect him from my father and this life. "I want you safe, but it's clear we'll be together anyway. We're stronger together."

"Then, that's my answer." He thrust inside me.

"Oh, God." I moaned as he filled my body. In just one swoop, I already teetered on the edge.

A low growl escaped him as he pumped once more inside me. His wolf was taking over, wanting to complete the bond as much as my wolf did.

I wrapped my arms around his body and dug my nails into his back. I'd had sex before, but this was a million times better, and we were only beginning.

Our bodies moved as one. His lips landed on mine, kissing me so much that I grew dizzy. The alpha inside me stirred, and I raised my hips, shoving him onto his back.

"Whoa, be careful." He chuckled and scooted to the center of the bed. "This isn't a huge bed. I almost fell off."

"Sorry, I just need to do this." I straddled him and

guided him back inside me. As I lowered onto him, he filled me deeper than before. That was exactly what I wanted.

I moved, and he matched me, proving we were connected in every way. I increased the pace, already close to the edge. I grabbed the headboard and used it as leverage. He slammed into me, deeper and deeper each time.

The urge to bite him and claim in all ways took over, but we couldn't do that, not yet. He needed more time. Our movement increased, and tension filled my body so much that it pushed me over the edge. I moaned as my body shook and I orgasmed harder than I ever had. Donovan groaned as he finished at the same time. As soon as the high was over, I crumpled against his body. Something inside me snapped and connected with Donovan.

"Oh, my God." He gathered me into his arms, pulling me against his chest. "That was amazing."

"Yeah, it was." I wondered if we could mind link together. Mates could do that, even if they weren't from the same pack. *Can you hear me?*

Uh … yeah, I can. Roxy connected with me. *Are you okay?*

Sure am. I sounded way too happy. *Just wanted to make sure the vampire hadn't shown up yet.*

Wait … She paused for a second. *You sound different … weirdly satisfied.*

That bitch was too attuned to me. Normally, I loved that she could read me like a book. It was usually a benefit when I needed a wing woman, but right now, it wasn't ideal. *I don't know what you're talking about.*

You hussy, she exclaimed. *You and he did the dirty.*

I should have been basking in the joy of my bond with Donovan, but no. I'd somehow connected with Roxy and was getting heckled. That summed up my life perfectly. *Okay, I'm tuning you out now.*

No, how was it? Roxy held on to the link, desperately trying to prevent me from cutting it off. *Was it as amazing as others have described it?*

Yes. Now leave me alone. I wanted to spend time with Donovan and not my bestie, reliving the moment I was still trying to enjoy. Maybe he and I couldn't link because we hadn't officially claimed each other with a bite, but I didn't want to freak him out completely. We'd pretty much completed most of the bond anyway.

Fine, but this isn't over, she grumbled.

"Are you okay?" Donovan asked with concern. "You seem unhappy all of a sudden."

"Yeah, sorry." I placed my hand on his chest and looked into his eyes. "Roxy is being annoying."

"Roxy?" He glanced around the room. "She's not here."

"We were ..." This would sound so strange, especially since we couldn't link. It had to be because he was mostly human. "... mind linking."

He chuckled then stopped. "You're serious, aren't you?"

"Yes, I am." How did I explain it to someone who would never experience it? "We're from the same pack link, so we can talk mentally. No phone required."

"You can talk to everyone back home?" He adjusted his head on the pillow.

"They have to be within a certain radius." I motioned to the room. "I'm far enough away that my dad can't keep tabs on me, so that's nice."

My phone buzzed in my jeans. I wished I could ignore it, but it might be Lillith or Katherine. I turned to get up and grab the phone when Donovan tightened his arms around me.

"We're supposed to be cherishing what we've just done," he chastised as he kissed my neck. "It's bad enough that Roxy popped in your head. I need your focus on me."

My body heated in response. If it was the vampire, she couldn't come into the dorm unless invited in. I moved my neck so he could reach it better. "I love your kisses."

"And I love kissing you." He trailed kisses down my neck, and a hand cupped my breast. "I don't know how, but I'm ready to go for another round if we have time."

That was our mate bond. From what I'd been told, newly mated wolves were locked in their bedroom most of the time. Hell, it didn't get much better even years later, but you managed to get your head on a little straighter. However, at first, with the bond so new, your wolves needed to connect as much as possible. It brought you closer mentally, physically, and spiritually.

"It'll be a hardship, but I'll make time for you." I tangled my fingers into his hair, enjoying the feel.

My phone buzzed again.

Maybe there was a problem. "I hate to do this, but I should check it."

"No." He lifted himself up and slid me underneath him. He captured my arms in his hands. "I won't allow it. Pay attention to me."

His head went back to my breast, and all my thoughts left me. All I could focus on was his mouth and tongue. "Oh God."

A loud knock on the door startled me, and his scent hit me square in the nose. There was no way he could be here unless he'd blocked the pack bond.

"Oh shit." I pushed Donovan off me, and he fell to the floor with a loud thud. I grabbed my phone from my pocket and opened the text.

It was from Lillith. **Mayday! Mayday! Tyler is coming in.**

My dad was here.

This was worse than the vampire. I picked Donovan's clothes off the ground and threw them at him. I mouthed the words "get dressed now." It would have been really nice if the mate bond had been fully functioning.

"Sadie." Dad's loud, commanding voice filled the air. "Answer this damn door now."

"Coming." The fact he was talking worried me more than anything. He had to be putting on a show for the humans.

I slipped on my clothes, and luckily, Donovan got dressed faster than me. I ran my fingers through my hair, trying to look presentable. I gestured for him to grab his food.

We had to pretend we'd been eating. Good thing sex had distracted us. At least, we wouldn't look as guilty. I took a large bite of my burger, walked across the room, and opened the door.

Dad stood there with a huge frown on his face. His salt-and-pepper hair was slicked back with gel like normal, and his matching goatee was neatly groomed. He wore a suit and looked impeccable, which was the gold standard for our family.

The vein bulging in his neck indicated how pissed he was, and only those who knew him well would have noticed.

"Hey, I thought you were coming tomorrow?" He'd wanted to eat dinner with Egan and me tomorrow night and stay overnight for the football game before heading back home. He was here a night early, which wasn't good at all.

"Change of plans." His eyes flicked right to Donovan,

who took a bite of his pizza. "Are you going to introduce us and invite me in?"

The stench of sex clung to the air. He probably already smelled it, but if he entered, he'd know it had been really recent. "We should go to the Student Center and get you some food."

"That won't be necessary." He pushed past me and entered the room. He sniffed the air and turned toward the human. "Who are you?"

"I'm, uh ..." Donovan started but then cleared his throat, unsure what to say.

"We were working on our biology project?"

"Is that what you call it?" Dad arched an eyebrow and looked down his nose at me.

At least, he wasn't beating around the bush. That had to be a good thing, right? I had to believe it was. I couldn't fathom the alternative.

"We have a paper due at the end of the semester," Donovan said, backing me up. "We were here to brainstorm."

"Is your paper on the various sex poses?" Dad dropped the bomb and waited to see how long it took to explode.

"Uh ..." Donovan stuttered.

"Can you stop?" He'd planned to make a scene from the start. "If you have something to say—"

"Just say it?" Dad cut me off and glared. "That wouldn't be very smart with him here, would it?"

In other words, Donovan shouldn't know anything about shifters or the supernatural world. "No, it wouldn't." I'd only told him about wolf shifters, not everything else, so I had that in my favor.

"I knew this was a bad idea." Dad scanned the room. "Not only are you here with *her*," he said, referring to Roxy, "but you make bad decisions. You better pack up. You're coming home."

"What? No." No way in hell would I leave Donovan. Not now. "It's the middle of the semester. I'm staying."

"I'm not sure what's going on here." Donovan stood and walked over to stand beside me. "But you can't just come here and pull her out because you don't like something."

"Oh, I can't?" Dad growled and took a menacing step toward Donovan. "I'm her father. I can do whatever the fuck I want. I don't need your permission or hers."

Dad would eat him alive. "Leave him out of this. You have an issue with me, not him."

"You're damn right I do." He walked across the room and got in my face. "You were supposed to come here to learn your place. If Brock wants you after this, it'll be a miracle."

"Want me?" I didn't give a flying fuck if Brock wanted me. "I don't want him, so it doesn't matter."

"Do you really think you have a choice?" Dad laughed and turned to Donovan. "Get the hell out of here. I need to talk to my daughter alone."

"No." Donovan shook his head, determined to stay by my side.

What a sweet and foolish gesture. "I'll be fine." I touched him, and my dad growled low. I dropped my hand, not wanting to make things worse. "Go on. It's okay."

Donovan glanced at Dad and then me. "Are you sure?"

No, I wasn't, but him being here was a very bad thing. "Yeah, I'll call you later." I had to appease him somewhat.

"Okay." He picked up his tray from the desk and paused. "I'll see you later, right?"

He worried that my dad would take me. It softened my heart even more. "Yes, promise."

"If you need me, just text." He looked at Dad and opened my door, about to leave. "I'll be here at a moment's notice."

I nodded, not sure what else to say. I took my phone and sent Lillith a text. **Dad made Donovan leave. Keep an eye on him.**

"You screwed a human?" Dad didn't waste any time before jumping in. "Are you trying to embarrass me?"

"Well, if you hadn't shown up unannounced, you never would've known." I needed to appeal to his logical side. "And I didn't mean for it to happen."

"How many times have I heard you say that?" Dad crossed his arms and glowered at me. "The time you tossed your wine all over Brock's face, or the time you allowed Roxy to attend an event with you and she hit on a fucking alpha heir."

There was no winning with him. "What do you want me to say?"

"Nothing." He waved his hand around the room. "You keep this mistake quiet so you don't ruin your chances with Brock. He already suspects you feel for this human."

"Why do you keep bringing up Brock?" I hated the douchebag.

"Because you're promised to him." Dad's eyes took on the alpha glow.

"No." That would never happen. "I won't mate with him." Hell, I was already a mated woman, but I couldn't let him know that. He'd kill him to get me out of the bond.

"Yes, you will." Dad closed the distance between us and stared me down. "You will align our packs to help me gain more traction among the supernatural races."

"No." I shook my head. There was nothing else to say.

"You will do this, or there will be heavy consequences."

Dad's nostrils flared, and his face turned a light shade of red.

"I don't care." I couldn't fathom being with that jackass even if Donovan hadn't been in the picture. "I'd rather die."

"There are fates worse than death." Dad stalked to the door and opened it. "Remember, this is on you since you defied me." Then, he walked out the door.

CHAPTER TWENTY-TWO

Dad's threat replayed in my mind. I wished I could yell at him to come back here, but it wouldn't do any good. Dad was determined for me to be with Brock, and he viewed Donovan as an obstacle. Even though our bond wasn't fully intact, it mostly was. There was no getting out of this gracefully now.

Hell, who was I kidding. Our relationship hadn't been graceful from the start. It had been bumpy and hard, which fit the story of my life.

I grabbed my phone and texted Lillith. **Did Donovan make it to his dorm okay?**

The seconds it took for her to respond felt like a lifetime. **Yeah, but your dad looked pissed. What the hell happened?**

The truth was too simple. **He caught Donovan and me.**

Her reply made me worry even more. **You're screwed.**

That put it mildly. I paced my room, feeling suffocated.

That wasn't new around Dad. He often held on tight and barely gave me room to breathe. That was why I'd been so surprised that he'd allowed me to come here.

Allowed me ... I sounded pathetic. Just a few minutes in his presence, and I was already the cowering little daughter he despised. Sometimes, I wondered if me being male would've changed anything.

I linked with Roxy, needing her to be aware before returning. *Dad's here.*

What? She sounded surprised. *I thought he was coming tomorrow. Did he catch you and Donovan?*

Pretty much. The stench of sex had been obvious. *Might as well have been in the act with how it smells in here.*

Wow, she deadpanned. *Now I'm so excited to come back home. That's the smell I really want to walk into.*

Staying in this room was driving me crazy, and her snide comments didn't make it any better. Maybe I needed to get out of my room and help the vampires keep a lookout. However, if I ran into Brock, that wouldn't end well. The best thing I could do was get some rest and stay put. I didn't need to piss Dad off even more.

I turned on the television and attempted to lose myself in a show.

ROXY ENTERED OUR DORM ROOM, startling me from my sleep.

"Okay, wasn't expecting you to be asleep." Roxy stifled a yawn.

"Me neither." I glanced at the clock and realized it was after eleven.

"Must have been all that sex." She waved her hand in

front of her face. "The stench is still strong in here."

I should've known she'd try to embarrass me. "Did anything odd happen?"

"No, it was eerily quiet after that shit show she pulled." Roxy sat on her bed across from me. "Egan is checking on Donovan before taking over the watch. Lillith and Katherine are going to take a nap."

My phone buzzed. I grabbed it and read the text from Egan. **Donovan and Axel are missing. Meet me outside my dorm now.**

"What's wrong?" Roxy's forehead was lined with worry. "Who's that from?"

"Egan." My heart pounded so hard it hurt. "Donovan and Axel are gone."

"Gone?" Roxy stood, and her voice rose. "What do you mean gone?"

"As in not in their room." I forced myself to take a deep, calming breath. They could've gone to grab a late-night snack, or maybe they were both in the bathroom. There were so many scenarios. "Egan wants to meet us outside."

"Let's go." Roxy crossed the room and opened the door.

I didn't need any further encouragement. I followed right behind her, and we were outside the guys' dorm within minutes.

"Where the hell is Egan?" Roxy scanned the area impatiently. "Nothing better have happened to them."

"Why do you care so much?" Sure, she was my best friend, and she would always have my back. But it was like she was as personally invested as me, which was odd.

"Because he's your ..." She stopped short. *Your mate.*

"No, it's more than that," I said, studying her, and she averted her gaze. She and Axel were at each other's throats. Could they be...? *Is he your mate too?*

What? Her eyes bulged. *No. That's impossible. He's human.*

I opened my mouth to push the conversation further, but Egan strolled out of the dorm. He was breathing so hard that I could see him inhaling and exhaling from here. He rushed right to us. "There's no scent of vampire anywhere in there, but that douchebag alpha who's been sniffing around you, he was out there."

"He lives there. The vampire's scent isn't there. That's a good thing, right?" Roxy's body relaxed. "That means they're safe."

"Their room was left in disarray." Egan's jaw clenched. "It looks like there was a struggle."

"They were fighting about me earlier outside the Student Center." My gut told me something was wrong, but I hoped I was being dramatic. "Maybe they had words."

Dad's whiskey scent and Brock's overly musky scent hit my nose.

My stomach dropped. No.

Dad called from behind me, "I wouldn't be so sure of that."

I spun around and faced him. "Did you do something to him?"

A smug grin filled Brock's face as they stopped a few feet from us.

"They're humans," Dad said carelessly.

"There could be—" I started, but he cut me off.

"There aren't any humans around." Dad scowled and gestured to the entire area. "If you were a smart or strong enough wolf, you'd smell them if they were near."

"That's not necessarily true." Egan came to stand by me on my other side. "Sometimes, you can be so preoccupied that something slips through."

"Like how the vampires on guard didn't notice me, huh?" Brock chuckled.

"What does that mean?" All sense of calm left. They'd done something to Donovan and Axel.

"Nothing." Dad glowered at him and turned his attention to Egan. "You're the elusive dragon, huh?" Dad held his hand out to him. "I'm Tyler, the reigning alpha over the packs."

The fact that he flaunted that title shouldn't have surprised me. It had been a long time coming.

"I didn't realize there was a reigning alpha." Egan didn't flinch. "From my understanding, there are hundreds of individual packs with their own alphas."

Anger filled Dad's eyes, but he smirked, trying to appear unbothered by the challenge. "That may have been true, but once Brock and Sadie mate, I'll have the leverage I need to have all the supernaturals under me."

"I'm not mating with him." He had lost his mind if he thought I would follow that order. "He's the last person on Earth I'd ever want to be tied to."

"Doesn't matter what you want," Dad growled and took a threatening step toward me. "I'm your father and alpha, and you will obey me. You had the chance to get out of it, but you didn't take it."

He was referring to Egan. Dad had wanted me to lock him in, but Egan and I were only friends. He deserved to be happy with his mate, and I wouldn't manipulate him for my own personal gain. I refused to be like my father. "I would not settle for anyone other than my fated mate."

"You don't have a choice." Brock laughed evilly. The prick was glowing. "You should be thankful I still want you after you fucked a human."

"That's awfully big of you." Roxy crossed her arms. "It

would be really embarrassing if she actually agreed to this. You being shown up by a human and all."

Brock's shoulders tensed. "What are you getting at?"

Roxy didn't back down. "That you act awfully conceited to make up for smaller things."

I couldn't hold back the smile, no matter how hard I tried.

Egan huffed with disgust. "You're going to stand here and let him talk to your daughter like that?"

"Why wouldn't I?" Dad frowned at the dragon. "She deserves it. She should be stronger than this. All she's doing is trying to ruin my reputation."

"No, she's not." Egan stepped closer to me. "She's trying to find herself and be happy."

"That's it." Dad pointed at me. "You're going home and never leaving again since you can't keep your head on straight. You obviously don't keep good company."

For the first time in my life, I stood firm. "No, I'm staying even if I have to find a job to pay for this."

"No, you're not." His eyes took on the alpha glow. "It's time I end all this foolishness. I've let it go on too long."

"What does that mean?" I couldn't believe that in a matter of twenty-four hours, my world had crumbled.

"This dragon isn't what I expected." He snarled at Egan and then Roxy. "These two are filling your head with stupid ideas, and I won't tolerate it. You are coming with me and never speaking to either one of them again. I refuse to let you fail me like your mother."

His words rocked me to the core. From everything I'd heard about my mother, she'd been strong and caring. If I was so much like her, then that was a compliment, not an insult. "No, I won't." I would not leave with him. "I'm staying here. Besides, it's too late. I already mated with someone."

Dad chuckled and tsked. "You think a human with a weak-ass wolf can stand in my way?"

How did he know? He'd only been here for a few hours, tops.

"Don't look so surprised." Dad sounded so damn arrogant. "It's my job to know what's going on."

"But that's impossible." It had taken me a few days before I realized that.

"There are many reasons why I came here with you." Brock rubbed his fingers along his shirt. "First off, I wanted to court you and do things properly, but that was a fail, so here we are. And secondly, Tyler expected you to do something stupid."

"Then, why let me come?"

"I hoped I was wrong and you would come here and be my dutiful daughter." Dad pointed at Brock. "You know I wanted the two of you together, but you didn't listen. I'm tired of suggesting. It's time I took matters into my own hands. You won't make the right choices."

"Those aren't the right choices for me." He had to see that.

"You think I care?" he asked condescendingly. "It's the right choice for me."

"You would make your daughter unhappy to get ahead?" Egan wrinkled his nose and shook his head. "That's disgusting."

"Now I know why dragons are nearly extinct." Dad blew out a breath, and his shoulders relaxed. "I was honestly worried when a dragon had popped up again, but it's obvious your strength has been overstated."

"It's not a weakness to care about those you love." Egan

puffed his chest. "It's narcissistic assholes like you who give it all a bad name." A low roar rumbled in his chest. "And maybe we aren't nearly extinct. Have you considered that? Maybe we aren't hiding but waiting for the perfect opportunity."

"Oh, please." Dad paused, but his arrogance snapped back in place. He whistled, and two of his guards appeared several hundred yards away from us with Katherine and Lillith in their grasps. "You can't do anything. I'll forgive you this one time for not respecting me as you should. After all, in a year, I'll rule over all the supernatural."

"Just let them go." None of them deserved to be treated like this. "They've done nothing wrong."

"Yes, they have." Dad scoffed. "They're fighting their true nature by choosing to be weak and pathetic. But not for much longer."

"Where are Donovan and Axel?" I asked desperately.

"You mean the two humans who keep drooling over you girls?" Brock sniffed. "They won't be a problem anymore."

"No..." I wanted to crumble, but I forced myself to stay standing. "What did you do?"

"I ..." He touched his thumb to his chest. "... didn't do a thing."

Of course he didn't. "Then, who did? The vampire?"

"That is one thing I do have to give you credit for," Dad said with some pride. "You found one of the oldest vampires in existence, and because of that, Brock was able to form an alliance between us and her."

My worst fear had been confirmed. "You didn't." I wasn't sure if Axel and Donovan being turned into vampires or dying was worse.

"Don't worry," Brock said and reached to pat my arm, but Egan stepped in, protecting me.

The alpha heir was intimidated enough to stop and drop his arm. "They won't be turned. I don't need a vampire getting in the way of my mate and me."

"What did I ever do to deserve this?" For the first time ever, I saw him for the true monster he was. He didn't care about me. I'd been foolish to think he might have. This proved he only loved himself.

"You caused problems for me and, worst of all, you were born female with pink hair." Dad closed his eyes as if it was too hard to look at me. "You will finally earn your keep as my daughter, but don't worry. You have time to say goodbye and watch the life drain out of that mutt." Dad grinned cruelly. "Don't ever say I didn't do anything for you. After all, that human mutt would've only held you back."

Donovan.

Nothing else mattered. I had to get to him. "Where is he?"

"In the woods. Follow the smell," Dad said. "Release the vampires. It's time they succumb to their true nature."

"You two, go back to the dorm." I couldn't leave my friends with him, and they didn't need to go to the site where Axel and Donovan would be and be tempted by blood. Either way, I was desperate to get to my mate.

"Oh, they'll go either way," Dad threatened.

"We'll be fine," Lillith reassured. "Let's go."

I knew I should push it, but I needed to save Donovan before it was too late.

Roxy, Egan, Lillith, Katherine, and I took off into the woods. Dad's and Brock's laughter enraged me even more than I was already. Thankfully, the sound vanished when we hit the trail, and I followed the vampire's sickly sweet smell.

"We need to be careful," Egan whispered, but Roxy and I ignored him.

I pushed my legs faster, and the trees flashed past me. I needed to get to Donovan and fast. Maybe I was being reckless, but I didn't care. If my mate was dying, I needed to be by his side. The fact that Roxy was just as desperate spoke volumes.

"There's no point," Lillith responded. "They won't stop."

The sweet smell grew stronger, and the metallic scent of human blood coated the air. With each step, it grew stronger and stronger. There was a lot of blood loss.

"Dammit." Katherine sucked in a breath and stopped.

It was enough to make me pause. "Are you okay?"

She shook her head, and Lillith grabbed her friend's waist.

"It's the blood," Lillith explained as her face became even paler. "We can't go any farther. We'll only make things worse."

"Are you okay staying here by yourselves?" I didn't want to leave them behind and then have them show up and lose their humanity.

"We'll head back a little so the smell isn't as strong." Lillith's teeth extended as she breathed shallowly, trying not to smell it. "Come on." She grabbed Katherine, and they took off back toward the school.

"We need to hurry." Egan caught up to us in seconds, and the three of us ran into the area where the vampire had attacked me before.

We found her leaning over Donovan with Axel right beside him. When she heard us, she straightened and looked at us. Blood trickled down her face.

CHAPTER TWENTY-THREE

"Took you long enough." The vampire licked the blood off her bottom lip. "I almost drained him completely before you got here. Do you know how much restraint it took me not to?"

"Get away from him now." One of us would die tonight, and I didn't care who as long as I could inflict as much pain as possible on the bitch.

"Aw, the pup thinks she can take me." She stood and stepped over Donovan's body like it was nothing. "How sweet. I may not even care that you're Tyler's kid when these two humans die."

"You won't hurt her." Egan stepped beside me and stared her down. "I won't allow it."

"Oh, like earlier today?" The vampire flipped her black hair over her shoulder. "I'm a little excited she made it through. I want to be here to watch her lose her mate. It'll be the icing on the cake." She kicked Donovan in the side.

He groaned in pain but barely flinched. He was already on the brink of death.

"Axel?" Roxy said, her voice shaky, but there was no response.

I had a feeling Axel had gotten involved by being with Donovan when it had all gone down. They were a package deal like Roxy and me.

Not bothering to let her gloat any longer, I rushed her, ready to kick her ass.

As soon as I reached her, she ducked, and I almost stumbled over her body. I dug my feet into the ground and halted.

I elbowed her hard in the back, and she fell. Holy shit, I could fight. My wolf guided me, protecting my mate.

Egan was beside me in a flash. He grabbed her by the waist, lifted her, and dropped her.

She hissed. "Do you think it'll be that easy?" She blurred as she ran behind us and kicked Egan in the back.

He stumbled forward, almost tripping over Donovan.

Let's attack her at the same time. I linked with Roxy. We needed to use our pack link to our advantage.

Good luck with that. Dad chuckled through the bond. *Neither of you knows how to fight.*

I didn't need his negativity giving me bad juju, so I blocked him from my link with her. *You go right, and I'll go left.*

Are you sure? she said with doubt.

Go. I wouldn't allow him to influence her. *Now.* We split up, and the vampire smirked, watching us attack her together.

"This isn't even a challenge." The vampire sounded disappointed. "At least, it's more riveting than the humans I hunt."

I would make that bitch eat her words. I darted right at her, aiming for her arm. Vampires could heal, but losing blood zapped them of their energy. That was their one weakness, other than sunlight if they succumbed to the darkness. If we could get her to bleed, it would give us the upper hand.

She'd expect me to go for the neck—the kill shot. That was my goal, but not at the moment. *Try to hurt her in any way. Arm, hand, leg ... whatever it takes.*

Roxy didn't respond, but she focused away from the vampire's neck.

I called my wolf forward partially, needing all her strength and abilities. As I lunged toward her, my claws descended. When my teeth were mere inches from her arm, I snarled. I'd managed a half shift, and I had no clue how.

"Oh, no you don't," she said and sidestepped me.

All I caught was air and skidded to a stop. I turned around right as Roxy attacked in her wolf form from the other side. The vampire dropped at the very last second, barely able to avoid Roxy's attack. She grumbled, "Ugh" as she crouched.

The vampire favored ducking over fighting head-on. That was good to know. As I overshot her, I clawed at her skin. The scent of sickly sweet blood filled the air.

Yes, I'd gotten her.

Egan's shirt ripped as he called his dragon forward. Olive green wings protruded from his back, and scales coated his arms and chest. He managed a partial shift where his middle half was beast and his head and bottom remained human.

He flapped his wings, flying low in the sky. He couldn't go too high or humans would see. Sometimes, keeping our presence hidden was more of a curse than a blessing.

"Don't get too cocky." The vampire held her arm, and her canines extended. Even though she tried giving off confident vibes, the prickly taste of fear faintly scented the air around her.

The dragon swooped down toward her, his pupils turning to slits. Smoke spilled from his nose as the fire within him burned.

I'd heard stories about dragon flame, but no one that we knew of had ever seen it.

"No." The vampire shook her head. "That won't work." She ran toward the bushes I'd been injured in earlier today.

Egan readied to blow the flames, but she had already jumped into the greenery. If he blew fire on her now, he'd set the woods on fire.

Sadie. Roxy leaned over Axel, tears filling the corners of her wolf eyes. *They don't have much longer.*

Egan had the advantage, and the vampire was hiding, so I ran over to her. Donovan's breathing was so damn shallow. She was right. If we didn't do something fast, we'd lose them forever. I lowered myself next to him.

Terror filtered through even though I needed a level head. Fear wouldn't do us any good. I didn't want to lose. I had to do something.

That's when the craziest idea hit me. *Roxy, bite him.*

What? Shock rang through our bond. *But they won't survive.*

Maybe they could. It was the only chance they had to live. *If we don't do anything, they'll die. What if this works?*

You're right. She nodded and lowered her head to his neck. *Please let this work.*

The sound of Donovan's heartbeat grew fainter, and the longer I waited, the more dangerous the change became. I wasn't sure if it would work since he was already part wolf, but it didn't matter. His supernatural healing abilities weren't kicking in, and the wound was fatal.

I gathered my courage and lowered my mouth to his neck. I nipped him, letting my wolf take over. I wasn't sure how to force the change.

My teeth oozed with a substance that tasted like chalk and saturated the bite wound. I wanted to stay like that for a minute to make sure enough of the substance got into him, but something hard slammed into my side.

A loud roar filled the air as Egan pumped his wings, heading in my direction.

The vampire grabbed my arm, turned me over onto my back, and pinned me to the ground. "I'm not a fan of supernatural blood, but I might make an exception for you." She lowered her mouth to my neck, going in for the kill.

I gripped the grass, and my entire body tingled. Suddenly, I was standing behind the vampire, no longer pinned to the ground.

"What the hell?" She glanced over her shoulder, her eyes wide. "How is this possible?"

I was wondering the same thing.

Using her distraction to his advantage, Egan swooped down, snatched the vampire, and flew into the air.

Roxy ran over to me. *Did you fucking teleport?* Her body shook hard.

Yeah, I don't know how. But we needed to focus on the fight. *Let's end this, for their sake.*

Yes, you're right, Roxy agreed and turned around just as Egan barreled down from the sky and landed a foot away from Donovan and Axel. He hit the ground hard, slamming her body into the ground. Her head jerked back at the force.

She grabbed Egan's arms. She extended her fingernails and pried them under a few scales. He groaned and jerked back, leaving blood flowing down his arm.

The bitch had ripped some scales off.

Needing to help my friend, I jumped to my feet and made my way over to her.

She stood on shaky legs as blood poured from her arms and knees. Between my claws and her hard fall to the ground, she was bleeding decently now.

"You'll regret this." She used her vampire speed, but the world slowed down around me. I lifted a hand, and something from inside smacked into her and held her in place. "What the hell?"

Fear filled her dead eyes, and she grunted as she tried to move.

Whatever the magic was that held her in place still poured out of me. I ran to her and punched the bitch right in the nose. A loud crack sounded in the small clearing.

Holy shit. Roxy ran over to me, her teeth bared, ready to fight. *You got her.*

"Sadie, be careful," Egan warned as he ran over to me. "She's old and strong. It won't slow her down as much as the others."

That was good to know.

She bared her teeth, despite the blood pouring from her nose and into her mouth. Her body shook with rage. "You aren't supposed to be this strong."

Yeah, I wasn't sure what was happening either, but I wouldn't question my abilities right now. We needed her dead and fast. "Surprise, surprise, Brock and my father underestimated me." But I'd spoken too soon because I lost whatever hold I had on her, and she stumbled a few steps.

"Don't get so cocky." She ran to the woods in a blur and turned around, holding the same damn gun as earlier. "None of you are stronger than a bullet. But before I end you three, I want you to watch your pathetic hybrids die right in front of your eyes." She pointed the gun at Donovan's head. "Not even your sad attempt to change him will work." She fired a shot, and I watched as the bullet raced toward him.

"No!" I screamed and held out my hand. The bullet stopped moving in midair and dropped to the ground.

"What the...?" the vampire croaked as Egan closed the distance between them. He breathed fire all over the vampire, and she screamed in pain. "No."

I turned my attention to Egan, worried he might need help, but the horrible image I saw would be seared into my brain for all eternity.

The vampire fell, crying in pain, but the flames only grew stronger. Her body turned black as she crumbled. Her pleas cut off, and her body began to ash. The smell of burnt flesh rocked my stomach, and I turned away and vomited on the ground. This was the worst night of my entire life.

"Get the guys out of here!" Egan hollered, breaking through to me, barely. "I'll take care of the fire. Just go."

The smoke funneled into the sky, but the horrid smell lingered. The flames were calming since it had rained earlier this evening, and the vamp was burnt to a crisp. I hurried over to Donovan, and luckily, his heart was still beating. It actually sounded a little stronger, but I wasn't sure if it was just my imagination. I couldn't lift him, so I grabbed his arms and slowly dragged him back toward the vampires. Donovan and Axel smelled a little more wolfy now, so the girls shouldn't be as tempted to drink their blood.

Roxy shifted and stood in horror, her eyes still locked on the vampire.

"Roxy, now. We need to get them out of the smoke, or Axel will die."

That snapped her back into the game. "Okay." She rushed over, grabbed her mate, and followed my lead.

I avoided looking at the dead bitch and Egan as we left the small clearing. I'd already seen enough and would have nightmares for the rest of my life. Even though that vampire had caused us harm, seeing someone die like that changed you, but I didn't need to focus on that. My mate needed me.

We were getting closer to the vampires. "Lillith? Katherine?" I figured Dad wasn't here, believing the three of us couldn't overtake her.

"Please tell me only the girls are here," Roxy whined but didn't pause. "I'm buck ass naked here."

The fact that I hadn't even realized that spoke volumes about our situation.

"It's me," Katherine said quietly. "Don't bring them closer. I won't be able to stop myself from feeding."

"We bit them." Even if they didn't survive it, at least we tried everything. "So you're good."

"Okay, let me check first." Her footsteps grew closer, and she appeared from behind a row of trees. "You're right. They don't smell nearly as delicious."

"Can you handle it, then?" I would hurt her to protect him if I had to, but I would rather not. "I don't want to fight you."

"I handled your blood earlier, and he smells a lot like that." Katherine came closer and grinned. "I'll be fine." Her face had color again, and her fangs were retracted.

My hesitation lessened. "Where's Lillith?" The fact that the older vampire was missing alarmed me.

"She went to get the car." Katherine pointed deeper into the woods and away from campus. "You know we can't go back there. Your dad will take you away or worse if these two survive."

"You're leaving us?" I tried to keep the hurt from my voice, but I thought we'd all grown close.

"No, silly. We're taking you to our nest. It's hidden, and only a few know where we live." Katherine placed a hand on my arm and looked at Roxy. "Uh... that's an interesting look."

"Shut up." Roxy grumbled as she glanced around. "I didn't have time to undress before shifting."

"Well, here." Katherine pulled off her black shirt, revealing a tank top underneath. "You can at least wear this."

"And be Porky Piggin' it?" Despite complaining, she gently dropped Axel's arms and grabbed the shirt, putting it on. "I guess it's better than nothing."

"Porky Piggin' it?" Katherine's brows furrowed. "What the hell does that mean?"

"You've never heard of that?" Roxy startled. "You know the cartoon character of the pig who only wears a shirt and no pants or underwear, right? That's what I look like." She gestured to her bare ass and legs.

Under normal circumstances, I would give her hell, but not now. We had to focus on saving our mates. "If you and Lillith go with us, you'll get more entangled ..."

"Not sure that's possible." She reached down to help me carry Donovan. "There's a nearby pack we're friendly with. We should be protected for a little while."

"But—"

"No buts." Katherine stared me in the eye. "We can't allow your dad to take control of the supernatural world, and if you go back, he'll use you to get ahead. We need to go. I can give them vampire blood once we're in the car. It should speed up their recovery."

I hated putting them into this situation.

"Sadie, please," Roxy begged behind me as she picked up Axel's arms again. "You got to at least tell Donovan how you feel and share part of our world with him. I didn't get the chance and regret it so damn much. We can't let them die. Please, let's go with them."

That's when the magnitude of the situation hit me right in the chest. They were right. I couldn't go back there, and if we didn't get our mates to safety, they would die. Hell, they probably wouldn't make it as they were. "What about Egan?"

"He knows." Katherine nodded. "We came up with a plan before he went looking for Donovan in case something happened. It's like the dragon knew shit was about to go down. He knows where the van will be. We just couldn't chance telling you until now."

"That's fair." My dad could get to my texts, and we'd been talking to him when they'd been dragged out by his goons. "Let's get out of here. Can you help Roxy?" Roxy wasn't as strong as me, and she was struggling to move Axel.

The three of us hurried as fast as possible, dragging the two humans behind us. We didn't want to injure them, but we weren't strong enough to carry them. It took longer than it should have, but eventually, we stepped out of the woods and found a large black van.

Lillith jumped out of the vehicle while holding some sweats and opened the door. "Let's get them in here. One can lie in the very back seat and the other in one of the reclined seats."

Beggars couldn't be choosers, so I didn't argue. As long as we got them out of here, that's all that mattered.

Lillith came up beside me, dropped the clothes on the ground, and picked up Donovan's legs. "Damn, he's heavy. That must be the wolf part of him coming out."

"Less complaining and more focusing." The more energy we wasted, the harder it would be to get him into the car.

After a ton of groaning and the four of us working together, we had Donovan in the back seat, with Axel lying in one of the reclined seats. He was lighter and easier than Donovan to put in that position.

The moment we got back out, Egan appeared from the woods. "Let's go. It won't take them long to come looking if they aren't already."

"Wait." We were missing one important piece. "Roxy, we have to remove our pack link with him; otherwise, he'll find us."

"Shit, you're right. But let me cover my ass cheeks first." Roxy blew out a breath and nodded as she pulled on the clothes that Lillith had been holding when she showed up.

"I'll give them some of my blood while you do this." Katherine climbed into the back seat.

"Okay, great. Let's do it." I took Roxy's hand and pulled her away from the car so we were under the moonlight. I wasn't sure how to do it. "We just need to reject him as our alpha."

Okay. Roxy linked with me. *How the hell do we do that?*

"Let's open up the bond. We'll have to go by instinct. Our wolves will naturally want to protect our mates." I removed the block from my father, and he immediately yelled in my head.

What the hell did you do? He was so pissed. *Get your ass back here now. The one time you decide to prove your strength, you kill a strong vampire. What the hell is wrong with you?*

No. I made sure my words were loud and clear. *I'm done letting you control me.*

Roxy, he growled. *You better get Sadie's ass back over here now.* His alpha will intertwined with the bond.

Your commands don't work on me any longer, Roxy replied.

I had no clue what she was doing.

Don't you dare, Dad threatened.

Sadie is now and has always been my alpha! Roxy screamed through the pack bond.

You will pay— But he cut off as the bond with him went cold.

A warm spot appeared in my chest that had never been there before. "Roxy, are you okay?"

"Yeah." She placed a hand on my arm and smiled. "I've never been so happy in my entire life, but what do we do next?"

My emotions were about to get the best of me. I'd never expected her to submit to me, but we had to focus on the most important step. "We save our mates."

But I left out the last piece because she wasn't ready to hear it—yet. We would get revenge on my father even if it killed me.

ABOUT THE AUTHOR

Jen L. Grey is a *USA Today* Bestselling Author who writes Paranormal Romance, Urban Fantasy, and Fantasy genres.

Jen lives in Tennessee with her husband, two daughters, and two miniature Australian Shepherd. Before she began writing, she was an avid reader and enjoyed being involved in the indie community. Her love for books eventually led her to writing. For more information, please visit her website and sign up for her newsletter.

Check out my future projects and book signing events at my website - www.jenlgrey.com

CPSIA information can be obtained
at www.ICGtesting.com
Printed in the USA
LVHW101142170722
723701LV00019B/160